# ELEMENTS
## OF VIOLENCE

Gilbert B. Bradham, M. D.

333 Confederate Circle, Charleston, SC 29407
843-364-6543

This book is fictional. All fiction rests upon real perceptions, so no fiction is completely unreal. And none is real.

Visit www.booksurge.com to order additional copies.

# Prologue

In the fall of 1981, an automobile abruptly changed lanes of traffic at a busy intersection. The vehicle was a 1968 Ford with multiple scars, and a dingy unkempt appearance. The motor, however, was quiet, the body did not rattle, and the tires were deeply treaded. The change in lanes was accomplished adroitly, as if by a race-car driver, pausing short of the intersection in a position that easily allowed others to pass. The driver carefully watched the passing cars for a minute and then swung the car into the traffic, maneuvered the intersection, and then abruptly turned into the back entrance of a small restaurant. The restaurant was closed, and the parking lot was empty except for one other car. The Ford circled the parking lot, its lights briefly illuminating all of the area. As the lights flashed across the windows of the restaurant, a large man could be seen hunched at the counter inside. He turned his head slightly as the lights reflected across a large vivid scar on his right face. After circling, the Ford came to rest in the far corner of the parking lot, and the driver emerged slowly, almost cautiously.

As the man stepped from the car, his appearance seemed consistent with his vehicle—faded and worn. He wore jeans, a sweatshirt and well-used jogging shoes. His face and head were hidden with disarrayed hair, gold-rimmed glasses, and a short thick grey beard. His stride and muscularity appeared that of a middle-aged athlete moving with confidence and agility. He walked directly to the other car, noted the license plate, make of the car, the degree of dew upon the window and top, and passed his hand over the hood and glanced at the tires. Between the car and the back door of the restaurant he watched the street, noted a cat near the garbage disposal, glanced at the sky with his weather eye, and finally inspected the side window of the restaurant through which one could see the dark shadow of the man inside.

The man who let himself in the back door was known to the police as Dr. Andrew Stevenson. He and the man inside were friends. He found the man hunched over a cup of coffee lazily watching the passing traffic. The man at the counter was police Captain Randolph Barringer.

"Hi, Andrew."

"Hi, Randy. How are tricks?"

"Up and down."

The two shook hands, then Stevenson found himself a cup of coffee from an insulated pot on the counter. Even in the almost darkened room, he managed his cream and sugar with familiarity and without effort or noise. When he settled on a stool beside Barringer, he sipped his coffee for a few minutes in silence. Both men faced the window, which commanded a view of the street. Hunched across the counter, each in his own momentary reverie, they appeared to be exactly as they were, familiar friends with certain similar interests. After a few minutes of settled reflection Stevenson spoke. "Do you remember the Borgni case?"

"Sure."

"I've been thinking about it."

"So?"

"I think we should talk to Borgni."

"Why?"

"He is the best example of uncontrollable hate and violence that I can think of, and I want to better know how he ticks."

"Why?"

"To construct educational programs on understanding anger, frustrations, and violence."

"What's the purpose of all that? What's so different?"

"We are entering an era of violence."

"Who says so?"

"I do."

"H'mmmmm."

The conversation was slow, each man carefully thinking out a response.

"Randy, its not different yet, but if our society continues to split apart into a philosophy of each on his own, it is intrinsically unstable and perfectly staged for conflict."

"Who is going to cause a conflict?"

"The blacks."

"You mean a racial thing?" Barringer's head came up to show a slightly incredulous expression."

"No. The blacks will exhibit the most violence, and the society will be programmed for misunderstanding the causes of violence."

"By what?"

"By having abandoned the church and the state."

"Jesus, Drew, you're weird."

"It's the truth, though."

"So what does this all have to do with Borgni?"

"I want to study Borgni."

"How?"

"I want to review his case and then want him interviewed by a specialist."

"You?"

"No, I want objectivity."

"What kind of interview?"

"I want to see under his skin. I want his background, feelings, early contacts, growth pattern. I want his guts."

"Andrew, is this some kind of personal thing?"

"No, I want to use him as an example. He fits. I'm thinking about a program on violence."

"Why?"

"To help focus attention on the subject. Maybe there's some way to approach the problem from a preventive standpoint."

"How?"

"Education. Begin teaching people about people from the day they're born."

"Drew, you always come back to that point. But I think you're missing human nature. People are always gonna be violent."

"I know."

"Why the push, then?"

"Got to give it a try."

The two men talked for a couple of hours. They talked comfortably, traveling from one subject to another, effortlessly. They selected the person who would interview Borgni and developed the general theme for the interview. They both knew the interviewer had his own style, but that if anyone could "get beneath Borgni's skin," their selection could. They sipped their final coffee as the sun began to change the parking lot from night's peculiar quiet charm to the tough reality of day. They shook hands and left, each forming his plan of getting a day's work done in an efficient, productive way.

Each set about to uncover events that had come to their attention in 1973, eight years prior. It had all begun with the murder of two young girls on a nearby island.

# Chapter I

On the southeastern coast of the United States, the city of
Detriville on the Atlantic Ocean contains a number of sea islands.
These islands vary widely in their length, breadth, soil, and vegetation.
The beaches on some of these islands contain a fine white sand, which
is a perfect carpet for barefoot children. These tanned children revel
on the beach, scamper among themselves, chase their puppies, and
laugh at the warm sun. The sun is not as warm on some islands. On
some of these islands, there is occasionally a strip of dark earth in the
beach sand, protruding ominously. Even the ocean waves appear rather
murky at times. These islands have fewer children. Each island is
unique, each having its own history, its physical individuality, its own
peculiar mood.

Pirates Beach is one of these sea islands. It is approximately
ten miles from Detriville and is sandy, possibly six miles long and
a mile in width. It was first used, as older people state, for evasive
operations by pirates. The pirates could tack their ships into the south
inlet where the winds are such that at almost a moment's notice they
could raise their sails and quickly slip out again into the reaches of the
Atlantic Ocean.

After the pirates were long gone, a bridge was constructed
to the island and roads were installed from one end to the other.
The people of the city came to build summer houses, many of
which remain. The old voices say that once it was a happy, beautiful
island. The beaches were clean, met the ocean evenly, were swept

daily by gentle breezes, and were warmed by the summer sun. Dunes supporting sparse reeds and bushes roll into a sandy backstretch that meets a line of palmetto trees and scrubby oaks. In the fringe of the tree line were built the summer houses kept cool by wind and shade. It is interesting that the old voices state that even in the bygone era of the island's social height, there was the feeling that the island held more sinister fate than was apparent to the casual observer. They say that at night there occasionally occurred a chill, a feeling of definite coolness, that was not quite consistent with the summer air, a sensation that all was not quite right within the island itself. Some say that it was the breath from the cold chest of one of the long-gone pirate men. Whatever that chill, it occasionally remains. There are those who would scoff at such a thought, and yet the island is now testimony to some vague unrest. Many of the old houses have slid into disrepair, for the island is now inhabited by working people who take advantage of the island because of its low rents and costs. Others still like the happier aspects of the island, particularly in the summer. Some live on the island in quiet isolation.

Albert Borgni lived on Pirates Beach. He lived at 903 Adams Street with his wife and two children. It was an uneventful family except for a few peculiarities. One of the peculiarities was the occasional appearance of Albert Borgni. At times his appearance was different, his mind was different, and his mind was responsible for his appearance. In 1973 he was thirty years old. He was exactly six feet in height and weighed 188 pounds. At most times, on casual inspection, his appearance was not striking. His body build was distributed evenly in a rather nondescript fashion, and he was not noticeable in a crowd. His hair was dark brown, almost black, and he occasionally wore a moustache. His skin was dark, as of Mediterranean origin, his eyebrows were relatively heavy and dark, his nose of conventional form, and his forehead expressed a slight perpetual frown as if he were concentrating. The mouth was humorless, the lips flat, unattractive, and somewhat compressed. His eyes were dark, and it was his eyes that mirrored the occasional intense chaos of his mind and soul.

Albert Borgni had a flaw—an intense hatred. He hated almost everything. At strange and totally unpredictable times, some abnormal area of his brain received complex signals from several circuits elsewhere in the brain. These signals acted to produce intense anger and hatred. Occasionally the hatred was not correctly interpreted by the rest of his conscious mind and became confused in fantasies and delusions. He hated, but did not realize he hated. The intensity of emotion at these times could be clearly read on his face and particularly in his eyes. When one looked directly into the eyes of Albert Borgni, he saw the result of human torment.

The structure of human torment is complex. The bounds of torment are not defined, and, in fact, that which torments one person does not particularly bother some others. What is apparent, however, is that if torment is carried on unduly, it gives rise to anger. If anger is continually involved, hate is produced. Hate is a powerful force and capable of driving men beyond control of themselves. It may be that hate or its tendency can be carried genetically.

Consider the relatively short period of time that modern man has been on earth. Consider early man. Imagine one named Onk.

Onk wakes in his cave after a restless and uncomfortable sleep. He ate too many roots for supper, and they have disagreed with him. First, the roots were unfit for human consumption, and secondly, Onk, as he so often does, ate them hurriedly in a rather unchewed fashion. As he awakes his belly and back hurt. He struggles to the front of his cave and frowns into the early sunlight. Something out there disturbs him, and he can't quite identify the problem. Lonely and with an existence that includes daily pain, Onk has learned to dislike many things. This morning the dislike has almost turned to hate. He considers killing something. As thoughts continue to occupy and perturb his primitive mind, he fantasizes beating to death an animal, or something.

Thousands of years later one of Ghengis Khan's men had a similar reaction. His name was Oochi. Oochi had ridden constantly for three days, and his poor little horse was near death. Oochi was tired beyond expression. The prior week he had been told to scout the desert south of the company and had became lost. When eventually he regained his bearings, he found that his company had left without him. Oochi had always felt inferior for the others were better soldiers, better horsemen, better lovers. Oochi had become lost, a shameful condition for a horse soldier. The little horse stumbled, fell, and did not appear capable of standing again. Oochi hated, for he could do no more. He stabbed the poor horse repeatedly until long after it died.

In Italy, several hundred years later, a soldier named Giorgio suddenly appeared quite insane and killed three women and two small children before he was subdued. The captain of the garrison had given explicit orders to maintain peace in the village and to provide a politically acceptable attitude towards the villagers. He had no option but to condemn Giorgio to death in order to satisfy the political conditions of the occupancy. It was of little moment anyhow, for Giorgio was not of value. Somehow he did not relate to his companions, was a loner, appeared to dislike everything. He was known to have had some strange difficulty with a young girl several years before and had not been trusted or liked by others since. As Giorgio waited for his death in his cell, he simply hated because he could do no more. Driven by his hate he managed to escape and kill again, for it was the only way that he could express his frustration.

Who is to say that the genetic code carried by Onk, Oochi, or Giorgio does not contain starkly irrational human behavioral patterns? Who is to say that the genetic code does not play Russian roulette and that sooner or later someone such as Albert Borgni inherits the traits of a combination of tortured souls?

Other theories exist. They describe imbalance in the mind. They state groups of brain cells in which exist both compatible and adversarial components, a balance of power. If by chance a set of these brain cells were to become over-trained, the balance of power might shift. In Albert Borgni's abnormal mind, it appears that some long-distant genetic code was handed from one inferior, belligerent person to another and finally became lodged in his brain. Another explanation is that some center in his mind had become the occasional dominant controller of his emotions. At most times there probably occurred a mental battle, a cauldron of hate, but one which only simmered. Perhaps forces gradually mounted and finally exploded into consciousness. These things are unknown, but what is known is that on occasion, a set of events begins to accelerate the simmering process and results in a boil-over. Rather than being perceived as a mental flare, the process is perceived as a fantasy or a set of delusions. When the delusions or fantasies are satisfied, the process reverts back to its original sickness.

Borgni had awakened early on a morning in May, 1973. Like the caveman Onk, many thousands of years ago, he had not slept well. He vaguely remembered a fumbled attempt at sex with his wife. He slammed a mental door on that recollection as he was apt to do with any inadequacy on his own part. The restless night was not explained on that one basis, however, for the night had included his morbid thoughts, the ones that often troubled him and made sleep restless. He vaguely remembered kicking at something. He remembered that the shape of the object was round like a ball or perhaps a human head. The recollection had another troubling aspect. It appeared in his dream that he had not only kicked at it, he had actually stepped on it, and when he did, it moved, so he had stepped harder, and harder, and it began to writhe and turn and twist and cry. It appeared to be wet. He tried to turn off this mental picture, but it troubled him.

He had been restless in his sleep, tossing about, dreaming frequently. Among his dreams of kicking at round objects, he dreamed that he was near a large lake, bordered by thick woods. He was chasing three white geese, and each time he caught one, he would try to hold it by standing on its neck. As soon as he reached for another, the one would slip from beneath his foot and run screaming into the woods. As he ran about wildly, several boys would appear and yell at him.

Around and around the lake he ran, the geese and the boys screaming, and beneath his foot he could occasionally feel a squirming neck.

He finally awoke, sweating, unsure for a moment as to his whereabouts. When oriented, he noted the time and knew that he would not sleep again.

After a shave, Borgni decided on wearing dark pants and leather boots. He did not realize the reason for which a particular set of clothes seemed to be appropriate at times, but the dark pants and white shirt were only occasionally worn, when they seemed to fit the need that he noticed on this particular morning.

His wife had taken the children to school and then had gone to her part-time job. She had left cereal for him, which he ate in an automatic fashion. He wanted a cigar after breakfast, but when he drove to downtown Pirates Beach, the cigar store was closed and he decided to drive to Detriville. He drove across the causeway towards Detriville, noting the egrets on a mud bank in one of the tidal creeks. The dream about the geese flashed back instantly. He felt a sudden sense of rage, wishing that he could catch and destroy the egrets. Far overhead two terns banked in unison, watching his car career angrily across the causeway, until he stopped at the Pirates Beach Road drug store to buy cigars. The saleslady was possessed of a remarkably sensuous body that she displayed in every way possible that a low-cut blouse and tight skirt would allow. While not apparently understanding Borgni's request, she straightened her skirt in a provocative way. When she finally brought his cigars to the cash register, she leaned forward to get a bag from beneath the counter, and in so doing, she gave a stimulating view of her breasts. Her smile met a sullen, dark face containing black pits for eyes that simmered with hate. As he quickly took his cigars and rapidly left, the cashier looked after him in momentary perplexity, wondering why she felt a sudden repulsion.

Although he had not intended to go to the Naval Base on his day off, he found himself on the way. He boarded the ship and looked through a number of photographs that he kept in a secured locker. After an hour of focused study, he left.

The rest of the day was spent in restless search for some unknown objective. Each time he stopped, he found people increasingly hostile to him, and he in turn became more and more resentful of having nothing tangible to do, no place to go, insufficient funds to spend on pleasure, and no friendships to rely upon. He became increasingly aware that people seemed to be noticing him. Each time he passed a police car, it appeared that the policeman was looking at him or his car. Once he noticed that a policeman was using his radio, and he wondered if he were the object of a call. He changed directions within a block and drove aimlessly for a while. He noted that the high schools were letting out in mid-afternoon, and found himself driving by one of the larger schools several times. The energy and the enthusiasm of the kids yelling at each other and chasing one another on bicycles angered him. Too much noise—they should be gagged. Once he watched a young boy and girl walking hand in hand. The girl was attractive, but the presence of the boy generated a sickening feeling deep within him, probably contributed to by the way the girl looked at the boy. With his mounting anger, his frustration became unbearable. He did not know what he wanted, and did not know any way to discover what was bothering him. He drove back to Pirates Beach.

As Borgni approached his home, he noted that his wife had not yet returned. He parked the car and did not go into the house. He looked at the beach and decided to take a walk.

Borgni crossed Adams Street at 4:30 p.m. He walked the path across the dunes by the side of 904 Adams Street. He knew the house was vacant but looked at it to be certain. The house had a door entering on the side and appeared to have a shower stall on the front ocean side. He turned eastward, and as he did so, he saw ahead of him a sight that brought him to a complete halt.

In front of him, playing and scampering like two young fawns practicing the rites of spring, were two pretty, fresh, joyful girls. They appeared to be in their mid-teens, were clad in white shorts and colored blouses. Both were barefoot, and they scattered sand in every direction as they kicked a large plastic ball at each other. They were about the same size, both appearing the personification of vigor and health. Both had rather long auburn hair, which tossed about like flags in the breeze. From a distance they could have been sisters, but on close inspection their lively faces were different and one was left with the impression of two devoted friends.

The impression would have been correct, for they had been companions since early childhood. One of them was Shirley Clair, was an attractive sixteen-year-old high school senior. Her long, dark brown hair hung in neat waves across her shoulders framing a calm, pleasant face. Today she wore a red, white, and blue blouse and white shorts. She was 5'7" in height, willowy and statuesque for a high school girl.

The other was Alice Lawton, slightly shorter than Shirley but weighed exactly the same, 110 pounds. She also had long, auburn hair, and wore an open, friendly expression. She wore an orange blouse and white shorts.

The Lawton's maintained a cottage at Pirates Beach, and Shirley was a frequent visitor. They had decided on a walk on the beach, hoping to be noticed by a boy who lived a block away.

"I'm going to leave my shoes here."

"I'll put my sandals over here, but remind me, Mom will skin me if I lose them. Ummmm, the sand feels good."

"Whose ball is that?"

"I dunno, but kick it down here."

"Maybe Ronnie is home."

"Could be. Did you hear who he went out with last weekend?"

"No."

"That girl from Brooks High who John used to date."

"Wow."

"He really did."

"Isn't this weather perfect?"

"Yeah, feels good, spring always does."

"Soon it will be summer."

"Yeah, Dad is trying to talk Mom into going to Florida, she wants to go to the mountains."

"Are you going to see that Bill again if you go up there?"

"Yeah, I suppose so, he scares me a little."

"Too fast too, huh?"

"Yeah, I guess."

"Gee, the beach feels great, like you could run forever."

"Did you see that?"

"Yeah, I've seen him before. Gives you the willies."

Borgni turned back towards his house. Inside of him a savage technicolor production had begun. Blues clashed on reds, purples were produced, blood spilled. His attention had frozen. His mind was set. A cold, calculated determination had occurred. The rest was automatic behavior.

He remembered his son's toy pistol on the sofa. Beneath the sink were a set of discarded drapes to be used as rags. Borgni carefully tore multiple cloth strips, rammed them into his pockets, and thrust the toy gun into his waistband. He then returned to the beach. He walked across the dunes and stood beneath a palmetto tree watching the girls from a vantage point some fifty yards away. They kicked the ball back and forth, occasionally letting it roll down towards the surf, following it, chatting pleasantly.

"So I told him that if he wanted to come out this weekend, that we might be here. He said that he and Charlie might get together and come out. They'll call tomorrow."

"Charlie said that he wanted to come out anyhow."

"Good, but I hope they'll both come."

The girls caught up with the rolling ball and nudged it back up the beach. Automatically they turned towards home. The shadows were beginning, and no one else was about. It is a natural phenomenon to set course for security before night provides doubt.

Borgni noticed the turn. He walked directly onto the beach, and turned directly towards the girls who still were attending the ball as they walked. Borgni stopped in their path. Shirley gave the ball a playful kick and the ball sailed beyond Borgni. She looked up abruptly, realizing his presence for the first time. Her mind had been filled with pleasant thoughts.

"Please excuse me."

The gun came out, Shirley stopped abruptly, looking at Borgni.

"Oh!"

Alice's breath came out in a gasp of complete astonishment.

"I have just committed a robbery, and the police are looking for me. You are to come with me. If you do anything to give me away, I'll kill both of you. Turn around and walk naturally towards that house. If you do not do exactly as I say, I'll shoot you in the back of your heads."

"Mister—I've got to go home."

"Come with me, little girls."

"Mister—please don't hurt us, let us go, we haven't done anything."

"Shut up and keep moving."

"Mister—I'm going to be sick, I'm going to faint."

"If you don't keep walking, I'll kill both of you."

Silence. Silence except for the soft crunch of beach sand, almost silent beneath the bare feet of two tearful, frightened girls followed by the audible and ominous sound of a man walking. The black leather boots left evil imprints in the sand, but time and wind would erase them gently as it does all things on a beach.

The trio walked towards the empty house at 904 Adams Street. The door to the shower room was partially opened, and Borgni herded the girls toward it.

"In there."

Alice saw that it was a shower room. Some intuitive sense engulfed her, and she turned to run. Like an animal stalking its prey, Borgni saw her intention almost before she realized it. He caught her arm with his left hand and essentially threw her into the shower room. Shirley merely looked at him with widened eyes and drained emotion. Tears streamed down her cheeks, but there was no sound accompanying them. They were the tears of fear and the realization of helplessness and dejection. Her head bowed and she turned and walked into the shower room.

Borgni put the toy pistol inside of his belt where it remained evident. Neither girl bothered to look at the gun. Alice was cringing against the far wall of the shower room where she had fallen, and Shirley had turned to face her abductor. Shirley's eyes were riveted on Borgni, the mouse transfixed by the cobra. Borgni latched the door and began taking the cloth strips from his pockets.

"Turn around. Put your hands behind you."

He tied Shirley's wrists behind her.

"Get up."

He pulled Alice to her feet and turned her to face away from him. He bound one wrist, then pulled the other backwards and bound the two together.

"Oh, that hurts, that's too tight."

He knelt and bound her ankles. As he rose from the kneeling position, he placed his left hand on the inside back part of her right leg and slowly moved it up along her thigh to between her buttocks.

"Please, mister, don't do that. Please let us go, we won't tell."

Alice burst into sobs, her entire body shaking with fear and dread.

Borgni placed one of the cloth strips in her mouth and bound it in place with another. She quit crying in an effort to breath effectively.

He then gagged Shirley and bound her ankles. He stood beside her pressing his body against her and placing his hand into her shorts. He would fondle her pubic hair and abdomen, then withdraw his hand and place the other into the back of her shorts and fondle her buttocks. He performed these acts again and again, each time holding her with his free arm. She trembled constantly, sobbing and choking into the gag, but was powerless to resist. The bound ankles prevented her from stepping away, and she simply had to allow her lower anatomy to be explored over and over.

Borgni gradually became excited. His rate of breathing increased, and he pressed himself more firmly against Shirley. He untied her hands.

"Take off your blouse and drop your shorts."

Her ankles were still bound. She had quit sobbing, realizing that she was going to be sexually molested, and wondering how and to what extent. She looked soberly into Alice's eyes imploring some type of help or advice. Alice stood still, unable to communicate and unable to comprehend. Borgni turned to her and untied her hands.

"You, too."

Both girls slowly, almost in unison, unbuttoned their blouses and let them drop to the floor. Each then undid more slowly the buttons and zippers of their shorts, and both stopped. They could not bring themselves to go further.

"Let your shorts drop down."

Neither moved.

Borgni reached towards Shirley, grasped the back of her shorts, and violently tore them downwards. Shirley toppled backwards to the floor breaking her fall with her hands, but uttering a muffled cry. Borgni moved towards Alice. She quickly slipped her shorts down to her knees. Borgni stepped behind her and rebound her wrists. He moved backwards and faced her.

"Spread your legs slowly and let your shorts fall to your ankles."

Trembling, Alice obeyed, slowly. The shorts slid downwards and as they did so she closed her knees again.

"No, open your legs slowly, open them. Open further. Now close them, slowly, now open them again. Now turn around and do it again, keep doing it slowly."

Borgni watched each muscle operate. He made her perform the act over and over. Finally he tired. He turned towards Shirley, reached down, grasped her by the arm and brought her back to a standing position.

"Undo your bra. Take it off."

He then tied her hands behind her and pressed himself onto her bound hands. With both of his hands, he massaged her breasts. He began active pumping motion into her hands and buttocks, but tired of this after a few minutes. He then went back to Alice, unbound her hands, made her remove her bra, and rebound her hands.

He aligned the girls side by side telling them that he would release them if they would do exactly as he instructed. He then sat down in a small wooden chair, which was the only furniture in the shower room, and unzipped his pants.

"I want you to touch titties. Rub them together. Again. Do it again. Now I want you to turn around and bend over. Further. Straighten up and do it again. Now I want you to turn away from each other and bend over. Stick your butts up in the air. That's right, no, more, that's better. Now squat down. Poke your chest out, more."

Borgni began to masturbate. As he neared a climax he had them both kneel in front of him. He ejaculated onto both of them. He wiped himself with one of the cloth strips and then smeared it onto Alice's face. Suddenly the atmosphere was changed. A violence entered as if the dingy shower room had been invaded by an electrical storm. Anger was present. Hostility rode into the room. He moved the chair beneath the overhead water pipes, and lifted Shirley onto the chair. He tied a cloth strip around the water pipe and then around her neck. He pushed her onto one edge of the chair where she balanced precariously. He repeated the same procedure with Alice. They faced each other trying to stay balanced on the chair. Their swollen, tearful eyes looking directly into their friend's eyes, both miserable, both trying to deny their present situation, neither contemplating the next moment in time.

Borgni looked at them with hatred and yanked the chair away.

As the bodies plunged downward, the pipe strained at the moorings, but held. There were two barely human utterances as two human windpipes were compressed by the weights of two bodies pulling against two nooses. Both bodies moved in jerking motions, struggling against the progressive lack of oxygen. The girls died almost simultaneously.

On Pirates Beach it seemed the wind stopped blowing, the surf quit pounding, the sand lay still, the sea oats stood quietly. There was no sound of bird or man or animal. The sky darkened just a little bit as death passed by.

A cold, icy feeling gripped Albert Borgni. His hate was gone and in its place a gnawing, growing fear. He looked at the two limp bodies hanging from the water pipes and felt the urge to move forward and release them, but did not. Instead, he fought a growing panic to run screaming onto the beach away from his disease, and from death and fear.

As time passed his fear gradually abated. Perhaps it followed the path of death across the sky over Pirates Beach. He rapidly walked back to his home, searched for a shovel, and finding none, seized a shingle that had recently fallen from the roof. He walked back to the vacant house. Kneeling in the sand in the rapidly gathering dark, he hastily dug a shallow grave. He cut the girls down from their nooses and buried their bound bodies in the shallow grave together. He dug another nearby hole and buried their clothes. He then threw the shingle onto the beach and went home. That evening the tide at Pirates Beach washed the shingle away forever.

# Chapter II

James Randolph Barringer was captain of the Investigative Division of the Detriville Metropolitan Police Department. He was called captain by his superiors when they tried to constrain him and Randy when they needed him. Both were common events. He was called captain by his own men when the situation became sensitive enough that they wanted him to be responsible for whatever events might ensue.

Actually, Randy Barringer was a very unofficial person. His division worked in a very unofficial way and used informality as an effective device. The secret was Barringer.

He had been born in a small southern town in 1934. He was the only child of rather exceptional parents. His father was a successful industrialist, and his mother was, in every sense, a lady.

He had everything that a boy in a small town could have. His early education was at a private school. He was naturally athletic, and his father furnished him with every available advantage to be healthy and strong. He was an excellent tennis player and fair in football and basketball. His mother had spoiled him somewhat and held to him as closely as possible. He was a quiet and rather sensitive child, serious and somewhat shy. The natural wear and tear of vigorous athletic programs produced in him a certain fairness, tolerance, and pleasantness.

After high school he attended a small but well-esteemed southern college, majoring in history and political science, but had the opportunity of electing a number of courses outside of his regular curriculum. He filled these spaces with a heavy load of seemingly non-related courses such as logic, philosophy, physics, and chemistry. By the end of college, he had decided upon law school and requested his father's support. His father was pleased with the choice and had his eye set upon a very prestigious school in the northeast. Randy, however, elected the state university in the state's capital. He told his father that the friends that he would make there might be helpful to him in the future.

Law school was not difficult for Randy, but he did not really seem to have his heart in it. After three years of law school and graduation in the middle of his class, he was faced with the need to finally set about making a living.

He was twenty-five years of age, appeared tall at 6'3" in height and weighed 195 lbs. He had slightly reddish-brown hair, dark eyes, an angular face, slightly bushy eyebrows, a hawkish nose and cheek bones high and sharp. His neck, arms, and legs were long and thin, though tough and muscular. His hips were narrow, and his shoulders were not unusually wide but were muscular and slightly stooped. He dressed loosely, casually. He appeared a rather perpetual student, shy and good natured.

After graduation he looked carefully at his state to find a relatively small town that needed a young lawyer. He balanced the social opportunities, school friendships, dating opportunities, and a library. Near the center of the state, only about thirty minutes from the capital, was the town of Dorchester. It was a well-appointed and neat town, unique in having attached to it a fair amount of industry, which gave it a sound fiscal base. He made his decision to attempt to practice law in the town of Dorchester and purchased a small wooden store across from the court house. It had been a grocery store for years but its owner had died and the store seemed destined to follow its master.

Randy spent his first summer as his own carpenter, and by the fall of that year the store had become one of the marvels of restoration in Dorchester. He had closed the front entrance and converted the front part of the store into two offices, the larger of which was his own and the smaller of which housed a receptionist-secretary. The back portion of the store had become his apartment and was suitably spacious and comfortable for that purpose. A small parking lot to one side permitted his clientele to enter a newly appointed entrance on the side, and he entered his apartment from the rear. The simple but attractive conversion had received acclaim and attention in Dorchester, especially from mothers with eligible daughters. The ladies' garden club made a visit to compliment him on the attractive shrubbery and unusual hedge that he had provided. Several were careful that their names were remembered and told him that they hoped that he could meet their family at some time in the future. The town welcomed Randy Barringer and made him feel comfortable, and he was pleased with his choice.

The autumn of his first year of practice was an easy slow slide into the world of responsibility. He had several interesting cases, although most of his work was the routine of wills, securities, and real estate transactions. He was not overburdened and used his free time in the pursuit of tennis and the out-of-doors. Quail hunting was a favorite recreation as was a late afternoon fishing trip.

Late that autumn he met Cassandra Lee. The Lee family was well known in Dorchester: Mr. Lee a successful businessman, Mrs. Lee the middle of the social circle, and twin sons who were the backbone of society and athletics in Dorchester. Cassandra was their pet younger sister. The twins were Randy's age, and their common interest in athletics and the out-of-doors had produced a congenial friendship. Cassandra, or Sandy as she was known, had finished college the year before and had moved to Arizona to take a job and live with her favorite aunt. During Thanksgiving she returned to Dorchester for a visit.

The twins had asked Randy to hunt with them during Thanksgiving and to have Thanksgiving dinner at the Lee home. The three men arrived clad in their hunting clothes, tired but pleased with their morning hunt. They sat in the library before a hot fire drying the morning moisture from their clothes, enjoying a cocktail before dinner. Mr. Lee brought Sandy in to meet the new young lawyer-bachelor. Randy was seated when they entered, he turned to see one of the most attractive women he had met. While obviously a few years younger than him, she stood straight and fairly tall and appeared remarkably mature and composed and confident. She was blonde with blue eyes, and the eyes twinkled with a kind of constant merriment. Her face was remarkably pretty but became beautiful when she laughed or smiled, which was frequent. A long graceful figure was draped in casual but singularly pretty clothes. He tried to rise but stumbled over the footstool and nearly fell. They all exploded in laughter while he blamed the twins for walking him to the point of exhaustion that morning. He was so immediately absorbed in Sandy that his usual grace and charm stammered into a rather senseless gibberish. The twins later laughed at Randy for his confusion. At dinner the Lee family enjoyed each others' company and Randy and Sandy enjoyed each other. Perhaps it wasn't love at first sight, but it was very close. He asked her out that evening and again on Friday. He took her to the state football game on Saturday and drove her to the airport on Sunday. The twins later took oaths that he did not shoot accurately on any future covey rise.

He tried to wait until her return at Christmas but melted halfway and flew to Arizona. They enjoyed a healthy weekend of quiet dinners in the evening and the vigor of the Arizona desert during the daytime. They wrote frequently until the Christmas holidays, when she took two weeks of vacation to return to Dorchester. They became inseparable in December. The holidays were filled with parties, athletic events, several trips on the pretense of visiting others in distant towns and even the pretense of wanting to see a new art gallery. They were obviously enchanted with each other and in such a state they were invited to every social event in Dorchester and among surrounding friends in the state.

Mr. and Mrs. Lee realized the intensity of the relationship and were pleased. The twins treated Randy almost as if he were a brother and were pleased to find someone who looked capable of taking care of their younger sister. The Lee home was opened to Randy. He and Sandy spent Christmas Eve there, decorating and placing gifts about the tree, greeting guests, and enjoying the solid closeness of a comfortable and friendly home. They treated it almost as if it were theirs. The Lees noticed and artfully left the couple to themselves. All retired early on Christmas Eve leaving the couple before the ebbing log fire, each in total comfort in the presence of the other. After Christmas the Lees gave a large New Year's Eve party, obviously done for the couple and the two were the center of attention. At midnight when the clock struck and the sirens sounded and all kissed and kissed, the crowd smilingly noticed that the couple were so oblivious that they did not realize that the sirens had quit.

The next day Randy and Sandy had a long talk at the airport. She wanted to be alone for a while. She wanted to think about him and their possible future. She stated that everything was too magical—that he was a magician who had placed her under a spell. They laughed but knew that they were caught in an explosion of emotion and pretended that a sober period of thought would be a mature way of approach to each other. They parted quietly, neither happy nor somber. He promised a visit in early March, and she promised to return in early April for a two week visit at home.

March did not come quickly enough. He re-packed his fishing gear and hiking clothes. He had packed it a month earlier at the time that he had bought his plane ticket. The wait until March had made him impatient but had been made at least tolerable by the planning of the long weekend. She was ready when he arrived, and they motored to an excellent fishing lodge in Colorado and spent blissful days together. They kept separate rooms, having previously discussed sex and physical attraction and mutually agreeing that their relationship was to be kept on as high a plane as possible. Their frankness with each other and their mutual determination helped both of them relax and truly enjoy each other. She had made her family aware of their regard for each other, and the family was comfortable with their frequent trips. The weekend in Colorado went quickly. She loved his enthusiasm for the streams and the fields, and he doted on her health and vigor and compatibility. They drove back to the city in Arizona in a quiet, thoughtful reverie. They both knew that the die was cast. He held her closely at the airport and had difficulty leaving her. They both poured out their hearts in letters that night.

She arrived in Dorchester in early April. On the second night after her arrival they went for a ride after dinner. Both knew it was time to discuss their future. He drove to a place overlooking a nearby river. It was a beautiful spring evening, no clouds, beautiful stars, and one could feel the freshness of early spring air.

He was a hunter and the first to hear a sound. As he turned from holding her, his car door opened. He turned to see a menacing man reaching for him and another approaching her car door. He instinctively attacked but stumbled on the foot pedals and lurched forward. A hand caught him and pulled him out onto the ground. As he gathered himself, stumbling to his feet, he was kicked in the groin. He fell to the ground in severe pain. Again he struggled upward. The assailant this time kicked him in the face splitting the right side of his face at the cheekbone. Unbalanced he fell onto his right side. The man lifted and brought down with intense force an iron lug wrench into Randy's left chest. The tenth rib broke into the spleen beginning a major hemorrhage. Once more he writhed upward. This time the lug wrench came down upon the back of his head, and he collapsed into the dirt, unconscious.

The second man had pulled Sandy from the car.

"Lady, he's dead. You do what we say."

They undressed her, pulling and tearing her clothes and throwing them onto the ground. They both assaulted her repeatedly, orally, anally, and vaginally. They beat her with their fists and left her a huddled wreck sobbing on the back seat of the automobile.

Somehow, later, she got into her torn and dirty clothes. She found Randy still unconscious but could not move him. She got into the car and drove home. Her family called the local sheriff and told him what had happened. They then took Sandy thirty miles away to a physician in the capital city. She was examined, given antibiotics to protect against venereal disease, was given a medicine to ensure against pregnancy, and a group of medicines for sleep and her emotional state. She was then taken to the physician's home, cleaned and put to bed. Several hours later she was escorted by her mother and father onto an airplane to Arizona and a private hospital.

The sheriff found Randy on his hands and knees crawling towards the highway. He was confused and in shock. They could not hold him properly to get him into a car, so sent for an ambulance. He was taken to a local hospital where an emergency operation was necessary to remove the lacerated spleen. His scalp was sutured, and the facial wound was found to be packed with dirt so would leave a bad scar. He had lost enough blood to be in shock but responded to transfusions.

Mr. Lee had returned from Arizona. He visited Randy and told him what had happened. He relayed the doctors messages that Sandy was not well and preferred not to see him again. Mr. Lee left little doubt that the family respected her wishes and that it would be preferable that they not consider a future relationship. The twins did not visit. He was left to himself for two weeks in the hospital. Even the doctors and nurses seemed too professional, and somewhat cool.

He was discharged after two weeks. The face healed poorly and was distinctly unattractive. No one visited his office. The receptionist stated that she had personal matters to attend and quit. The town was distinctly distant.

Randy Barringer considered his options carefully. He sold his office-apartment and returned to his parent's home. He carefully researched opportunities in the armed services. He enlisted in the Army requesting the Special Forces. He would be inducted in early June leaving him almost six weeks at home.

During that six weeks, Randy lived almost entirely to himself. He discussed non-personal matters with his mother, was courteous to his father, but not close. He ate by himself most of the time, and if the schedule produced a meal with his parents, he was generally silent. He rose early each morning and began a grueling day of exercise. He ran increasing distances at increasing speed. There was an empty football field at the fairgrounds. He performed all of the exercises of a football player but at an increased pace and at an increased length of time. He played tennis against himself on the side of a vacant building. He worked himself into the capacity to hit the bell so fast and with such force that it seemed that he was intent upon exhausting the ball rather than himself. He paid dues at the local YMCA and used the exercise room at any time that he was not elsewhere punishing himself physically. In the exercise room were weight-lifting and muscle-building equipment. There were light and heavy punching bags. He worked at the bags relentlessly. His physique was not that of a typical boxer and when others occasionally came through and watched him, they naturally wondered at the reason for his aggressiveness. At such times the jagged scar on his face was purple and gave others an uneasy feeling. He lifted the weights until exhausted. He ate food only to survive, he bathed to wash away the sweat and pain of exercise, and he went to bed only when he was so tired that he could not help but fall asleep immediately. He arose early each morning and began it all again, and again, and again.

At the end of six weeks he was a coiled spring.

He had requested the Special Forces as an Army discipline. He had asked a family friend in the United States Senate to intervene if there were any difficulty getting the choice. When time came, there was no difficulty so it appeared that he was either fortunate or the friend had intervened. He had been interviewed by Army psychologists as to his selections and his reactions appeared plausible. He appeared to be cool and collected and offered no evidence to suggest that special training would be inappropriate. Shortly after induction he was sent to a special camp to begin his training in the Special Forces.

On the second day of his training, he and nineteen other recruits were assembled for their orientation into the techniques of hand to hand combat. They were to be given a karate demonstration by selected instructors. Divided into groups of twenty men, they assembled around a large mat to be lectured by an instructor who would also demonstrate basic techniques. The protocol for such demonstrations included instilling into the new recruits a substantial respect for their instructors. Such respect was an effective substitute for discipline. Unfortunately, it included scare tactics, which were relished by the instructors and often had far-reaching effects on the recruits. Robinson was Barringer's group instructor. He was a black man in his mid-twenties, muscular, experienced in warfare, and an expert in karate. After a harsh talk intended to subdue the new recruits, he stated that he needed a volunteer to demonstrate a point. He selected a large muscular but somewhat awkward and slow black recruit.

"Come on nigger, you're in the Army now. Pull your razor and try to cut old Sergeant Robinson. Don't you have your razor? Come on, try to box old Sergeant, come on nigger."

There was a nervous chuckle in the group of recruits. It disappeared when the big black recruit tried to swing at the Sergeant and was thrown across the mat landing heavily and awkwardly.

Possibly slightly embarrassed by the recruits' ineptitude, Robinson tried again. He hoped to select one with a little more aggressiveness and enthusiasm.

"You there, raw meat, you, the ugly one. Someone cut up your pretty face? My, that's the ugliest face that I ever saw. Come on out here. Come here, boy. You stand out here with me. What's the matter? You scared of me? Come on over here. I want you to hit me, hit me as hard as you can. If you can't hit, kick. Do anything, ugly man, but try to do something."

He was a bit perplexed with Barringer. Randy had walked out to the center of the mat and simply stood there looking at Robinson.

"Hey man, you scared of me? Don't let my rank worry you. I want you to try to hurt me. I'm gonna cut your white ass one way or the other. Better try to get a lick in before I hit you first. Hey, man, how did you get that ugly scar? Somebody slap your silly little face?"

Robinson reached with his left arm to slap at Barringer's right face, the side with the scar. Randy stepped forward with his left foot and swung his right arm. By the time he hit Robinson it was coiled into a super tight fist. When it hit him it was probably traveling 60 mph, and by this time had a straight arm, shoulder, and tensed body behind it. He hit Robinson at about the sixth rib beneath the left armpit back of the muscles of the chest. The force broke Robinson's sixth rib driving a jagged edge of the rib into the left lung puncturing it. Robinson began falling towards his right side. Midway in the fall, Barringer's left knee rose in an accelerating manner crashing into Robinson's right face. The blow fractured the right zygomatic bone and the maxillary bone which make up the cheek and upper face. Robinson's head snapped up from the blow and again began its downward decent, unconscious now. By this time Barringer's right fist slammed into Robinson's left jaw breaking the mandible or jaw bone. Barringer stepped back and aimed to kick at the remainder of Robinson's battered face.

Sergeant LaRue had been fifty feet away at the edge of another mat lecturing a similar group of recruits. Perhaps his peripheral vision had seen Barringer standing in the middle of the mat. Perhaps he had heard Robinson's taunts. No matter what senses made him aware, he had wheeled about at Barringer's first blow. He was running when the knee came up, crossing the edge of the mat when Barringer stepped back to kick. With the many options available to him to maim or kill, LaRue elected to merely throw his body at Barringer. He had been running hard, and the crash sent both men down. LaRue spun in mid air after hitting Barringer, put down an arm expertly, rolled on his shoulder and was back up like a cat. Barringer recovered less speedily. The two men now faced each other. Again LaRue could have charged while Barringer was gaining his feet but again his senses instructed him differently.

What kind of man was this, this tall bony awkward man with the bad scar on his face? His stance was not karate, it wasn't anything, yet there is Robinson down on the mat bloody and perhaps dead. What the hell was this? His hands are not trained, and yet here he is looking at me as if he could care the hell less.

LaRue circled, keeping Barringer off balance and constantly having to change position. LaRue noticed and knew that he could attack at any time and probably be successful. He also noted the lieutenant approaching from the side.

Lieutenant Callas approached the two men. Robinson was down in a bloody heap on the mat and LaRue was measuring a recruit, a big guy with a bad scar on his face. The guy was calm, and LaRue was collected. The other recruits had stepped back and were quiet.

"LaRue!"

"Yes, sir!"

"What the hell is going on?"

"I don't know, sir. Robinson is down."

"You, did you do that?" He pointed at Robinson.

"Yes, sir."

"Why?"

"He told me to."

LaRue relaxed. Lieutenant Callas was better than any of the instructors under him and he could handle the recruit. He walked over to Robinson, knelt down beside him, and noted that he was breathing, although he seemed to be breathing unusually fast. He had a good pulse. He noted that his mouth was full of blood so he left him on his side to allow the blood to flow out onto the mat. His right eye seemed to protrude and his face was rapidly becoming swollen. He called to

Jones and told him to go for a medic, now. Jones knew something had gone wrong and raced to the hall, made a call for emergency medical help.

Lieutenant Callas talked quietly with Barringer. He found Randy to be calm and rational and was told that the Sergeant had instructed him to damage and he had obliged him. Callas asked him if he resented the instructor or disliked blacks or was angry about anything. Randy simply stated that he was not. Callas then told Randy to return to his barracks, clean up, and remain there until he received further instructions. The lieutenant then went over to Robinson and remained with him until the ambulance arrived.

At noon, Sergeant Jones came for Randy and escorted him to the captain's office where the captain and Lieutenant Callas awaited. The interview with the captain and the lieutenant lasted almost an hour. They had his personal folder and went over the details of his background with him. They then asked him where he had learned to fight. He told them that he had not learned to fight. They asked him why he requested the Special Forces. He told them that it seemed to be a good outfit. They asked him why he had volunteered to join the services. He told them that it seemed like a good thing to do at the moment. They asked him why a college-trained lawyer would want to be an enlisted man. Randy told them that he did not want to be responsible for other people. They asked him a thousand questions, his answers were bland and noncommittal. After a long interview, the captain looked very carefully at Barringer and the notes that he had made during the interview. He was quiet for an unusual length of time. He then simply asked Barringer if he would like to volunteer for special training. Without asking what it was Barringer looked at him straight in the face and replied in the affirmative. They assigned Barringer to an accelerated course through the Special Forces and wrote the incident with Robinson off as an accident.

He received extensive training at a special school and was then sent to the Ranger School. He finished Ranger training and was sent to Vietnam. He traveled the length and breadth of Vietnam generally by himself. He was like a ghost, appearing and disappearing according to his own schedule. He was loosely attached to several units for supply purposes. He became an invaluable source to multiple intelligence units. The intelligence units loved him as he produced unusual and highly creditable information. They saw that he had credentials to go anywhere that he pleased and be supplied at will. He was not demanding of much but helped himself as he considered necessary. Only a few times was he confronted, and at these times his attitude became so intense that others considered that he was better left alone. They noted that he was unique among the Rangers by wearing an orange stripe on his collar but they did not understand what it meant and did not question him. They simply noticed that he had a rather jagged scar across one cheek and that when he looked intently at you it gave a sense of distinct uneasiness.

He was discussed widely but no one knew enough truth about him and his ventures to establish him as much more than a mystery. He was a hunter ranging far and wide and many times only at night. He was known to keep his equipment in excellent order, and it was noted that he used an unusual amount of ammunition and grenades. It was not unusual that when he returned in an early morning that his clothes were bloody. He was frequently sent to bring in prisoners, and it was a peculiar habit that he never bound their hands. He seemed to thrive on danger and appeared to dare anyone to a serious confrontation.

He had hunted the North Vietnamese relentlessly. Toward the end of his tour, it appeared that he was becoming gradually more like a human being and less like a tiger. He maintained his night patrols but appeared to be more intent upon gathering information than on wreaking havoc and death. Toward the end he quit with war and began to look at the country, its people, and its history. He spent several weeks in Saigon relaxing and then took his time getting back to the States. He visited throughout the East, stocking up on camera equipment and attractive artifacts. He had saved sufficient money to send his parents some attractive gifts.

He visited Hong Kong and toured extensively in Japan. He was growing increasingly more friendly and the Easterners took well to the tall Ranger when he grinned and smiled. They were cautious if the smile was not there, but he appeared to reserve his moody moments for his own kind. His mood improved. He entered conversation more easily. In an unboistorous way he drank with others of his ilk and gradually readjusted to civilization. After vigorously satisfying himself with Japan he returned home.

During the last few months of his duty, he instructed and lectured on special techniques of clandestine warfare. He minimized killing techniques and maximized the use of information gained by forward observers. He instructed on the recognition of important information, the organization and transfer of this information with Intelligence Services.

In the winding-down process, he began the planning of ideas that might contribute to his return to society.

He designated a period of time to spend with his parents. During this time he put away his war mementos. He took out fishing rods and backpacks and returned to his native out-of-doors. He renewed his tennis. He dated when the opportunity arose but did not pursue one direction for any length of time. He set aside two final weeks in the Caribbean to "bake the devil out of himself" as he put it.

On return, Randy Barringer made an appointment with the chief of the Detriville Metropolitan Police Department. He drove down to the coastal city and interviewed with the chief. He told the dhief his wartime experiences had left him restless and that he did not desire to return to law practice. He asked for the opportunity to join the Metro Force and work his way into some responsible position. He mentioned his interest in intelligence work.

The chief nearly bit through his cigar. Here was a bona fide lawyer from an obviously nice background asking for a job as a rookie. After his suspicions cooled, he instructed Randy on the steps necessary for training and work. He told of the low pay and the few fringe benefits. He reminded Randy that police departments contain an almost military discipline.

Randy listened patiently and answered quietly and genuinely. He began his basic training at the Police Academy six weeks later. He used his six weeks to work as a police cadet and to read everything available concerning police work.

He set a record at the Academy that has never been equaled. Only in the physical hand-to-hand techniques did he back away to some degree. He stated that he had already been trained in these techniques and did not desire to hurt himself or anyone else. He demonstrated that he could deal with others in a manner that did not require his needing to render them helpless. In all other matters he excelled. At the end of each day when the others were tired or griped, he read. The Academy had a good library, and during his six months there he read a good portion of it. The instructors liked him and offered occasional special learning opportunities. He took all opportunities. His fellow trainees seemed to realize that he was different from them, but it made them try harder to get along with him. They both gained from the endeavor. He had opened up a good bit by now, his big casual grin had returned, and as he allowed himself to become closer to the others it was found that he was a natural leader among them.

Toward the end of his basic training, he and the others were allowed out of the Academy more often in the evenings. He returned to friends of his law school vintage. They were amazed by his selection of occupations but promised to be helpful. Dates and social life were arranged, and he began to participate in pleasant affairs with his friends.

In the next few years he rose progressively through the police ranks. He did his stint at each level, but as soon as the time commitment was complete he took the next examination and advanced himself. His advancement was rapid.

When he became lieutenant, he began dating a Detriville girl. They had met on a blind date. Her name was Jenny Storer, and she was a nurse at the Metropolitan Hospital. She was a pretty, black-haired, dark-eyed girl who was of a serious, no-nonsense type of demeanor. She had struggled to gain her education and had worked hard to become a head nurse in one of the large sections of the hospital. They liked each other and began arranging dates suitable to their busy schedules.

He asked Jenny to marry him on the day after he made captain. They married quietly among family and close friends. Thereafter, she saw to his well-being with pride and diligence. He, in turn, saw to her every comfort and assured that she was always safe and well-protected.

Randy Barringer matured as an excellent police officer. His diligence and devotion to his profession, his pursuit of detail, and assurance of cases well-prepared earned him respect and esteem.

# Chapter III

On the day after the disappearance of Shirley and Alice, the Pirates Beach Police Department officially requested assistance. Detective Bartey interviewed the girls' parents. Both sets of parents were ideal in their care and concern for their girls. Neither home had any apparent friction, and certainly did not seem to warrant runaway status. The girls appeared to have been exceptionally happy and were emotionally stable. Their school friends and their teachers were interviewed by Detective Bartey. None of these interviews produced information to suggest runaway status. For some reason, the television media kept suggesting the possibility of runaway status, and the majority of people who heard of the case appeared to assume that they were runaways. Apparently for that reason, the case began to die out as a community concern.

As the days passed after the disappearance of the girls, one family became increasingly depressed and agitated. They sought daily information from the police and appeared disconcerted when they heard nothing new. They bought time in the local newspapers and offered a one thousand dollar reward for information. Shortly afterwards, the girls were supposedly sighted on three occasions. A couple reported the girls hitchhiking and gave identical descriptions to the missing persons report. They stated that they saw the driver of a commercial truck company pick up the two girls on a North Detriville highway. State Police stopped the truck at the state border and found that the trucker had two teenage girls who he had picked up at the reported site. Both were dressed in blue jeans and one of the girls was black.

Later there was an anonymous telephone call of the two girls being sighted in San Francisco. That proved fruitless. There was another anonymous telephone call stating that they had been killed and buried on Pirates Beach. Detective Bartey had the Air Force perform overflights of the island and make ultra sensitive infrared photographs hoping that these would be revealing of grave sites. These efforts were not successful. He then had police auxiliary units combined with Boy Scout Troops literally search every square foot of the island for grave sites. The electronic sniffer device was extensively used, and the State Police brought in blood hounds. No grave sites were found. At this time, one family contacted a psychic in Belgium who mailed back a map showing the location of a grave site. The area indicated was extensively explored but with no positive findings.

No positive clue was provided as to the true nature of the girls' disappearance. With no real clues, Detective Bartey and his squad had accumulated a list of possible suspects.

Detective Bartey's squad listed twenty-two persons to be investigated relative to the girls' disappearance. Two had died and sixteen of the remaining twenty were ruled out in the Clair/Lawton disappearances.

Of the four suspects remaining in the Clair/Lawton case, two had records and a history of violence, one had been accused of sexual abuse, one of child abuse and one was a chance suspect. The two with records were Joe Rasin and Pedro Pasquale. Rasin was a white male, age thirty-three, lived on Pirates Beach, and had been convicted of armed robbery and burglary with assault. He had misdemeanor records of bar fights and had used a baseball bat on a victim. He lived with a common-law wife, was a physical-fitness habitual, and frequently was seen jogging on the beach. There was no positive connection with the Clair/Lawton disappearances, and he offered no substantial alibi.

Pedro Pasquale was a twenty-six-year-old Mexican American. He lived on Pirates Beach with his wife and two children. He had a record of aggravated assault with a deadly weapon. In prison he had been considered to be a prime suspect in the killing of two inmates who apparently sought to abuse him. He could not be proven to be the killer despite the fact that several inmates apparently witnessed the killings. He was considered to be extremely violent, especially when drinking. He was a construction worker and had been with one company for several years in Detriville. He apparently did all right when on the job, but was given a wide berth when drinking at local bars. He was especially prone to violence when taunted about his heritage or looks. He was considered to be the person responsible for nearly amputating the arm of a college student several years ago over an innocent joke in a bar. Detective Bartey questioned Pasquale and attested to his tendency towards violence. It could not be established that Pasquale did not have the opportunity to be involved in the Clair/Lawton disappearance and he, therefore, remained as a suspect.

The sexual abuser was a forty-one year old white male named Howard Slade. Slade had never married, was suspected of homosexuality, and had been previously charged with sexual abuse of a child. He maintained a summer residence on Pirates Beach. The charge of sexual abuse occurred four years previously when he reputedly lured a young boy into his home and abused him sexually. The boy broke away from him, but either fell or was pushed down two flights of stairs on the outside of the house in his attempt to escape. The fall was seen by the boy's father who was looking for the child at the time. Following the child's hospitalization, the father attempted to kill Slade but missed him six times from fifteen feet with a .38 caliber revolver.

Many offers had been made to teach the father how to shoot more accurately. Bartey had interviewed Slade and detested him.

The fourth suspect is a twenty-seven-year-old white male carpenter named George Brown. Brown lived alone in a small home in the 1200 block of Pirates Beach. The house was owned by his father, who was a respected merchant in Detriville. George had been in trouble most of his life. The parents bailed him out for years until George caused a very bad disturbance at home and insulted his mother. The father allowed him the house at the beach but nothing more. George was a martial arts participant, had been violent at times, and was apparently unpredictable. He lived from hand to mouth by doing minor carpentry jobs. Detective Bartey investigated Brown's possible involvement and could not establish a connection with the Clair/ Lawton disappearances.

A psychological profile had been requested from a consulting psychiatrist. It suggested that if the girls had been killed, that their killer or kidnapper might be living on Pirates Beach. He was probably a single man, although being married with a family was not to be excluded. He was probably a pleasant, helpful, quiet type, who was generally likeable. He would probably be somewhat moody and tend to be a loner, but when he wished could be an intelligent, communicative person. He would tend to avoid conflict and argument. He probably had reason to hate his mother. He probably had been abused in some way as a child. He would be a person unlikely of being suspected of kidnapping and murdering a child. He might be additionally hard to find because his deeds might be random and unplanned.

When the psychiatrist was asked what driving force might lead to this type of kidnapping or murder, the psychiatrist replied, "Anger and hate." When asked at what, the psychiatrist had answered, "Anything."

Nothing was gained from the suspects, and no valid information led to the missing girls.

# Chapter IV

On the nineteenth of September, 1973, four months after he had killed Shirley and Alice, Albert Borgni felt uneasy. It was one o'clock in the afternoon. Borgni had lunch at 12:00 and had tried to nap afterwards. He had almost dozed off when he felt as if he was being engulfed by ocean waves. He sat up and found himself covered with sweat. He lit a cigarette, smoked for a minute, and then walked out onto his front porch. He stood there trying to understand his inner perturbations. It was a pretty, early autumn day, sunny and warm, not hot. In the autumn Pirates Beach was more quiet than on a summer day. The crowds left on the day after Labor Day, leaving as if some magnetic force impelled them back to their cities and farms. The birds and citizens of the beach were always glad to see them go, and September was their reward. September at Pirates Beach was still summer in terms of warmth and sunshine, but it was more pleasant due to the trade of warmth for heat and quiet for noise. There was almost an air of nostalgia, a sense that the busy summer was over and now there was a time of reflection and reverie.

Borgni was confused. Some sort of memory kept attempting to surface and seemed to have about it an exciting air and yet somehow was tinted with a sickening harshness. A few minutes ago when almost asleep, he had felt as if he were in the ocean. As a giant wave seemed to wash over him, something in the water touched him. Was it a hand or a piece of cloth? He shuddered and quickly suppressed the struggling memory. An impatience seized him. His family was away. He and his wife and he had not gotten along well recently. She was continually disturbed by Albert's growing nervousness, excitability, and mounting confusions. His memory, in particular, seemed to be under stress. As he would struggle to remember an event, some grotesque set of circumstances would tend to surface to replace any pleasantness. His wife had recently recalled a nice day spent in the sun at the lake near Brandon, Massachusetts, some five years previously. As he smiled at the returning memory, three white swans suddenly attacked him, one of which was covered with mud and spattered with blood. He had shuddered and gripped the railing of the porch for stability.

He scanned the beach not knowing what he was seeking, but sensing that something had to be overcome. He turned abruptly and strode forcefully into his bedroom, disrobed, pulled on heavy black socks, noticing, as he pulled up the right sock, the round scar on the outside of his right calf. He dressed in the dark pants, the black pointed boots, and the black jacket. He paused to light a cigar and then walked out of the house onto the beach.

Dori Jean Weatherby spread a blanket on the sand of Pirates Beach. She slipped off a white cotton blouse and tan shorts that had covered her two piece black bathing suit. She placed the clothes adjacent to her pocketbook and sandals, and then knelt, looking at the ocean and smoothing her hair. Dori was a sun worshiper. She had learned her religion as a young girl at her father's side in the fields of their farm. Her father was a large, rough man who adored his little girl and took her everywhere. As the father had worked the fields, the little girl would eventually perch on the wagon or a hay stack to feel the warmth of the sun. There she was, a golden princess ruling over all the daisies, all the sunflowers, all the birds and beasts. There she smiled in her reverie, imagining herself to be a lady of the court. Often she would sing little snatches of songs taught by her mother. They probably originated in some court long ago, possibly in the Elizabethan England the little girl saw in her sun-filled dreams.

She left the little farm after high school to try to succeed in nursing school as her only hope for further education and development. Her early years of deprivation and self-reliance stood her well. She learned quickly, capitalizing on a natural ability to help others and to gradually harden to the difficult clinical tasks expected of her. She possessed a peculiarly well-constructed sense of balance. She knew she was pretty and attractive, and knew her ability to be a woman. She knew intuitively her capability to balance her assets to gain from others in the professional and social worlds. She was willing to give, but aimed at a fair return. Her sense of balance was extraordinarily keen, and she succeeded. She was highly respected in the nursing school and actually regarded as a bit of a prodigy. She was given clinical assignments ordinarily reserved for those of greater experience. She performed her work capably, caring for patients with a firm and positive hand, and yet providing the sufficiency of individual human kindness required by the sick. In her social world, Dori chose carefully, selecting intelligence and promise rather than the flashy momentary favorite of the crowd. She learned the social graces by quiet, careful observation of those to whom these courtesies had been given by birth. She was a good-looking, healthy, strong young woman with a growing confidence. When she occasionally tired or began to have even the slightest doubt of herself, she came to the beach to be re-energized by the sun.

Still in a kneeling position, she looked out to sea for a long time, her mind entirely vacant. Gradually she felt the warmth of the sun upon her face. As she realized the first pleasant glow of warmth, she almost laughed but suppressed the laugh and simply smiled. She closed her eyes and turned her face upward to the sun oblivious of all that was earthly. As the sun radiated its heat onto the lovely face of one of its favorite children, Dori felt herself as a little girl again, high on her father's wagon, singing a child's song in pleasure. Her lips barely moved in memory, her shoulders relaxed their mature confidence, and she became a young girl again for a moment.

When she opened her eyes, a man was standing about twenty feet away staring at her. He was dressed in dark clothes, and was wearing pointed leather boots. As she opened her eyes, he quickly walked away. She stiffened with an uneasy feeling of apprehension. Dori really did not recognize fear, having never really been unafraid. Lightning and thunder, darkness and muffled noises in the night had been the constant companions of her childhood, and nothing had ever hurt her. She commanded, she was confident, but the figure walking away had, for a fraction of a second, given her a distinctly uneasy feeling. Perhaps it was his eyes. They appeared to almost register hostility. She suppressed the thought and turned to her blanket to enjoy her day with the sand, the surf, and the sun. She lay for awhile on her back gathering in the photons sent through thousands of miles of space by the nuclear explosions of the sun. As she warmed, she became sleepy, thought of her work and of her future, social promises, of negotiations, and of spontaneity. As sleep tempted her, she rolled onto her abdomen and stretched an arm beneath her cheek.

Borgni thrust the barrel of the toy pistol down onto Dori's temple.

"Get up and get moving, or I will blow your head off."

Dori was fully awake. Her training to be immediately aware of another person's sicknesses, apprehensions, fears, and acute changes of condition helped orient her bearings.

"Get your clothes on."

She was acutely aware of the gun. Despite his apparent intention to provide fear, she remained unafraid. He confused her. She perceived the aura of intense concentration on her. He did not appear to be concerned with anyone or anything else. She stood up and pulled on her shorts.

"Hurry up. I've killed two policemen, and I'll kill you."

She was puzzled. What did killing someone else have to do with her? She buttoned her blouse and considered running. She glanced up to see if anyone was within screaming distance.

Borgni saw her eyes search the surroundings.

"Put on your shoes, pick up your pocketbook and start jogging this way. One false move, and I'll shoot."

She noted the tone of his voice. It had changed slightly. She tied her sneakers and again considered sprinting. It was the gun that provided the decision. She reasoned that she could talk to him, but the gun might go off if she chose the wrong strategy.

They jogged eastward on the beach. Dori noted that there was no one else on the beach. Two boys were playing in the surf, but she did not want to involve them. The man ran beside her, the gun now in his jacket pocket.

"Turn here."

He directed her toward a green, wooden beachfront house. A boardwalk stretched across the dunes to meet stairs to an upper front porch.

Borgni directed her through a door beneath the stairs into a downstairs room.

"Lie on the couch face down. Put your hands behind your back."

He tied her wrists with insulated electrical wire. He then tied her ankles.

She considered talking to him, of trying to reason with him, and decided against it. It appeared to her that he was becoming more nervous than she was. She decided to bide her time and try to understand his motives.

Borgni produced two dirty white rags from his jacket. He folded one and tied it about her eyes, blindfolding her. He tied the other tightly about her mouth, partially gagging her. He was breathing hard now and had a growing sense of panic. Somehow things were not going well. He had not realized how mature she was and how apparently stable she was. She did not appear afraid, was not begging, was not whimpering, had not pleaded, had not even asked him a question. Something was wrong. The familiar torrent of hate had not arisen as had been consistent on previous occasions. She lay quiet and still. Her eyes had closed as the blindfold had been applied. Hers were not the wide, questioning, panic-filled eyes of abject terror nor the tear-filled eyes of young, complete helplessness. Borgni felt a sense of panic.

"Get up. I'm taking you in the next room."

She swung her legs off the couch and placed her feet on the floor.

"Stand up."

She stood up. As he pushed and guided her, she hopped in the direction of his push.

"Stop."

He opened the bathroom door.

"Hop forward two steps."

She hopped.

He took a third piece of electrical wire from his jacket and adroitly tied it into an effective noose and slipped it over her head. He glanced upward at a ceiling pipe.

Dori felt the noose about her neck and sensed its purpose. She struggled against the gag and mumbled loudly.

Borgni was startled. He slipped the gag loose to try to understand what she was saying.

"What do you think you're doing?" she said. "Take this rag off my eyes."

Borgni slipped the blindfold off.

Dori glanced about at the bathroom and then looked squarely into Borgni's eyes.

"Why are you doing this?"

"I just robbed a store. I shot two policemen. I'm waiting for my friend to pick me up. You're my hostage."

Dori knew he was lying.

"You don't look like you've shot anyone. Are you hurt?"

"Look lady, you don't know the danger you're in. I might kill you. Do you want to live?"

"Yeah, I want to live, and I think you do, too. Are you hurt?"

"No. How old are you?"

"I'm nineteen. I'm a nurse. Why do you want to hurt me?"

"I don't want to hurt you. You're my hostage, and I can do anything with you that I want to."

Borgni held the noose cord with his right hand and moved his left hand over her breasts. He let the cord go and unbuttoned her blouse. He pushed the blouse onto her arms. She glanced away and for the first time he detected the possibility of uneasiness on her part. With her arms tied behind, her breasts were prominent. He untied her halter straps and let the halter fall to the floor.

"Now do you understand that I can do anything I want to?"

Dori carefully calculated her answer and replied in exactly the tone she wanted to transmit.

"Yes, I understand."

Hers was a husky voice, deep with emotion, but not of fear. She carefully controlled all but her femininity. She knew she was taking a calculated risk, but she knew that now was the time to play all of her assets.

Borgni grasped the noose with his right hand. He fondled her breasts with his left hand and would bend over and lick and suck her nipples.

She intentionally began to breathe more heavily and began to twist and move in a limited fashion. She turned more against him than away. He stood upward and looked at her carefully. She returned his look and then glanced down, not in fear, but almost provocatively. Borgni reached into his pants pocket and produced a folding knife. He slowly unfolded it in front of her face. Her expression did not change, but she looked at him rather than the knife.

"I'm in control, and I'll do anything to you that I want to."

He began placing the back of the knife blade against her abdomen and then her breasts, across the upper chest, beneath her arm pits and around her neck. He rested the knife on her lips.

She looked at him and said, "Let me ask you something."

"What?"

"Would you like to make love to me?"

"Yes."

"If you will take this thing from around my neck and untie me, I'll promise you not to run or fight, and I'll make you feel real good."

Many of the human feelings are companions. Certainly fear and anger are close. Laughter and sadness are so intermingled that little children often burst into tears when unusually funny occurrences happen. Greed and generosity are almost inseparable at times. One can almost detect despondency on the miser's face when he places his offering in the church platter. Pride and humility are somehow so associated that a person truly inbred with one is considered a paragon of the other. Great athletes exhibit pride and humility simultaneously. However, of all human emotions that travel the paths of expression and the roadways of human direction, love and hate are the most frequently interspersed.

Borgni knew intuitively that for some reason that today's unusual circumstances were depriving him of his usual sustenance of hate. The expected hate simply did not appear. He did not know whether it was the maturity of this captive or the fact that the captive was not degraded. For whatever reason, he could not muster the destructive surge of hate that usually accompanied these circumstances. He removed the noose and untied her hands. She removed the blouse and let it fall to the floor. He bent down and untied her ankles.

She unfastened her shorts but let him strip them downwards. She did the same for the bathing suit bottom, and, as he bent down stripping it to her ankles, she turned her body toward him, holding her abdomen an inch from his forehead. He stood up as she stepped from her bathing suit and both of them looked fully into each others eyes. With careful timing, Dori turned and walked over to the couch and lay down.

Borgni completely disrobed. The round scar on the right leg caught Dori's attention. She quickly shifted her gaze neither acting provocatively not looking fully away. Borgni attempted intercourse, but as she prepared to accept him, his partial erection fizzled. After trying again, he got up, and Dori partially turned away. He tried to stimulate another erection by masturbation. Unsuccessful, Borgni stood up, walked over to his clothes, and began dressing. She turned toward him and watched him dress. He looked at her and realized that she did not contain apparent ridicule, fear, dejection, or any emotion except calm.

"If I let you go, will you tell anyone?"

"No."

"Swear?"

"Yes."

"Why?"

"No reason to."

"You're not mad?"

"No, I'm a nurse."

The answer appeared to satisfy him.

"You got a cigarette?"

"Yeah, hand me my pocketbook. I'll light one for you."

She lit two cigarettes, handing him one. He sat down on the foot of the couch, pensively looking at her. After a minute, he dropped the cigarette, stepped on it with the pointed boots and stood up.

"I'm leaving. Don't move for fifteen minutes. Remember, I've still got the gun."

"Oh, by the way, what's your name?"

Borgni had turned to go. He turned back and looked at her. It appeared to Dori that he had agony in his eyes, but then, this time she didn't care. It was her time to hate, but she controlled it.

Dori slowly dressed and sat on the couch again, considering options. Exactly fifteen minutes later, she stood up, took a deep breath, walked through the door onto the beach, looked up at the sun, smiled sadly and walked down the beach to her car. She drove straight home.

Two weeks later, Dori accepted a lunch invitation at the Naval Base. Lieutenant Daniel Miller was one of her favorites. While an Annapolis graduate and of healthy physique and medium good looks, he was shy. She had met him at a church function, noted the shyness, and had taken time to talk to him in a manner that allowed him to respond easily. They had become close friends, each eager to share with the other problems, ambitions, and joys. Dori accepted most of Dan's invitations because he appeared so grateful for her company.

The Pine Room at the Naval Base was a favorite lounge and restaurant. The lounge portion was suitably arranged for quiet conversation. The restaurant portion had a counter and tables, relatively low lighting, and the best sandwiches made in the area. Dori and Daniel sat at a far corner of the counter discussing plans for the spring. Daniel mentioned the probability of his visiting his home in Massachusetts and tried to portray the trip in a way that might involve interest on Dori's part.

Dori enjoyed Daniel's pleasure of reciting things that were familiar and comfortable to him. She even considered the possibility of asking him to let her go with him. As she started to interrupt him, she glanced at the doorway to the lounge and saw Albert Borgni.

"Daniel, I want you to listen carefully to me."

Dan quickly looked at her, startled by the tone of her voice. He found her looking intently into his face. He had never seen the expression she now wore. Her face was grimly set, her eyes hard, her lips clenched. Alarm grew in him. He could not fathom what had produced this sudden change, this unfamiliar countenance, the interruption, the almost unfriendly tone. His face reddened, his voice stammered.

"Sure."

"Daniel, I'm going to have to tell you something that I would not tell anyone else. I don't want you to interrupt me, I want you to pay careful attention. I want your help. I want your strength and friendship right this moment like I've never wanted it before. I want you to listen to me quickly without moving one muscle and then to advise me. Promise me you'll do just as I tell you without moving."

Dan was completely confused. His response, however, was born of his natural abilities, an innate calmness, a capacity for contemplation, and the ability to promise and keep his word. He sensed a need on Dori's part, and he braced for it. His shoulder straightened, his arms shifted, he intertwined his fingers, and he looked carefully into her eyes, seeking for the meaning of the change.

"A man has just walked into the lounge who assaulted me a couple of weeks ago. Don't turn around, I'll show him to you in a minute. He's apparently going to buy a beer. He's standing at the bar in the other room. I'll tell you when to turn around. He didn't rape me, but he tried to. I was out at the beach, and he stuck a gun in my face and made me go with him to a vacant house."

Daniel stiffened. "I want to see him, Dori."

"Okay. He's the one standing at the end of the bar with the blue jacket on, the one with the black hair and the small moustache."

"What happened, Dori?"

"He had a gun and a knife. He made me undress, and he tried to rape me, but he couldn't."

"Did he hurt you?"

"No."

"What do you want to do, Dori?"

"I want to kill him."

Daniel looked at her carefully. She was watching Borgni. Her face was grimly set.

"Do you want me to go for him?"

Dori remained silent for a long time, intently looking at Borgni. Finally, she looked back at Daniel.

"I think we should go for the police. Would it bother you?"

"No, I'll stick with you on anything."

His tone was the deciding factor. The strength in his voice and his obvious unalterable devotion could not be denied. She knew she could do anything that was necessary, and his compliance and help would only make it easier. Daniel placed more than enough money for the lunch on the counter, and they walked out together leaving by the restaurant door. Halfway down the block they stopped at the military police station and asked permission to call headquarters on an urgent matter. The MP on duty dialed the numbers, and Daniel explained the nature of the problem. The naval base police arrived, and Dori explained the events of the Pirates Beach encounter and that her assailant was in the lounge. They entered the lounge together, and Dori pointed to Albert Borgni. As he was apprehended and turned toward her, he showed absolutely no recognition. Neither spoke.

Borgni was placed in one police vehicle, and Dori and Daniel in another. On arrival at the naval police station, Dori gave a complete statement of the incident at Pirates Beach. She waited on the typewritten copy, carefully read it, and signed it. Borgni was meticulously questioned. He denied all involvement and appeared grievously confused by the entire account. He admitted living at Pirates Beach and taking occasional walks on the beach, but stated he had never seen Dori Weatherby in his life. He attested to his marriage and children and stated he had no need of other affairs.

Dori was carefully instructed in the legal aspects of her complaint by a Lieutenant Shatner. She was told that she was a civilian who was stating that an assault had been performed on her while on non-government property. As such, the U.S. Navy had no jurisdiction in the matter. She was told that her complaint must be made to Magistrate W.S. Simpson at Pirates Beach. She was told that Magistrate Simpson would be in his office at 10:00 a.m. the next day, that he would in all likelihood issue a warrant for Borgni, the Pirates Beach police would arrest Borgni, and that the complaint would then begin its way through the legal process to finally arrive in a court of law. Lieutenant Shatner then stated that he had explained the full extent of the law as was proper. He asked permission of both Dori and Daniel to express a personal opinion. They accepted.

"The man Borgni looks like an odd duck to me. I will bet good money that he will not confess to the assault. It will come down to your word against his. With no tangible proof, you will have a hard time winning this case. You will have invested time and money, exposure and a nasty court scene to gain very little. Somehow I believe he is going to hang himself eventually. I would bet anything that he will not try to bother you again. You might do well to let it go. I know you hate to, but at least consider it overnight."

It was mid-afternoon by the time Dori and Daniel left the police station. Borgni had been released and had gone. Dori and Daniel drove up the coast to a fishing village. They had dinner at a small seafood restaurant and drove back later to her apartment. They talked until late. Daniel stayed that night at the apartment sleeping on the sofa. She got up early the next morning, fixed breakfast, and prepared to go to work. Before leaving, she hugged Daniel tightly. She kissed him for the first time. She kissed him too warmly for a mere friendship. She then left for the hospital. She worked hard that day, putting an extra effort into everyone's care. She made no attempt to contact Magistrate Simpson.

Daniel Miller floated on a cloud back to the Navy base. His men wondered if he had lost his mind.

# Chapter V

Lieutenant James Pierce was second in command in the investigative division. He was a large man who knew every fast food restaurant in town. He listened well to the many contacts he met over hamburgers and coffee with an easy affable manner of extracting information. He also listened well to Barringer and learned from him at every opportunity. He had the job of attaining Barringer's instructions and relaying them to the others in the division.

Sergeant Robert Bartey had been severely abused as a child. He had been raised by foster parents in a mountainous community that was rife with family feuds and constant trouble with existing law. His foster father had been an extremely violent bootlegger and had used Robert as a virtual slave. Ruthless beatings with straps and sticks, words and whips had been the rule. His foster mother fought back with Robert caught in the middle. Robert's upbringing had been blood and death, toil, incest, and insult. He had burst away as a teenager running eastward until checked by the ocean. Making his way down the East Coast, he found a job at the YMCA in Detriville. The director at the Y had the physical attributes of the foster father but none of the verbal or abusive characteristics. The director seldom spoke, and Robert adopted silence. Within a year he was back in school and living at the Y in the afternoon and at night. Unable to compare with any classmate, he set about using every physical facility and class that the Y offered. By the end of high school he was a gymnast, high scorer at basketball, a weight lifter and master of the martial arts. He remained quiet and unobtrusive. When award banquets were given, he was not present. A classmate would hand him the award the next day and for a moment Robert's eyes would say "thank you" but generally his lips did not move. After high school had been completed Robert Bartey frequently went back to watch his alma mater play football. One evening the game was one of rivalry with a school noted for its rough student body. Robert had sat through the first half perched high in the stands and out of the way of trouble. During the half he was on the way to the snack bar when a fight developed. Caught in the melee, he found himself unable to escape three gang members. A knife flashed, and a body crumbled. A pipe rose quickly but descended slowly, accompanied first by pain and then by unconsciousness. A fist struck and when missed, found the bony support of its arm broken. Robert melted into the crowd of awed spectators and was quietly headed for the exit gate when a hand seized his arm. Reflexes responding to what he thought was his fourth attacker, he swung a well-trained kick only to find empty space. As his next move began he felt his other leg hit by a better aimed kick than his. Halfway to the ground he was caught again by surprisingly strong hands. He was forcefully spun off balance and was powerless. When he stopped, he was caught with one arm pinned behind him in a firm but painless fashion. He was looking into the face of a man with a huge scar across his right check. Ten feet away a lady stood patiently.

The man spoke to the lady. "Jenny, you drive, I'll ride in the back with this young man." The man then turned to Bartey. "I am Captain Barringer of the Detriville Police Department." Jenny then drove to their home. Barringer had taken Bartey in the kitchen and told him to sit down. There had been no other conversation, no search, no request for identification, no pleasantry. Jenny had taken a pie out of the refrigerator, placed it on the table and had retired. Barringer had made coffee and shoved Bartey a cup. Bartey had sat quietly touching neither the coffee nor the pie. Barringer ate slowly and refreshed his coffee.

After approximately thirty minutes, Bartey looked at Barringer and said. "What do you want?"

"Nothing."

Silence.

"Why am I here?"

"I thought you might want to talk."

"I don't have anything to say."

"Why not?"

A long pause.

"Just don't."

"Everybody got something. That's some of the best defense I've ever seen."

Bartey's eyes came up. "Defense?"

He found Barringer smiling and looking at him carefully.

"Yeah in my book that was defense."

"Then I'm not stuck with anything?"

"No, you are not stuck with anything. In fact, I was wondering if we could work something out."

Only years later after rookie training, the Academy, the advanced training, did Barringer tell Bartey that he had checked him out weeks before having wondered about the sad, silent kid high in the stands by himself game after game.

Bartey was the expert on violence. He worked all of the violent crimes quietly. He had been working with the Pirates Beach missing persons case since it had begun.

Rodney Canthus was medium build, slim, and almost delicate. He had blonde hair, a wisp of a mustache, florid clothes and a gold chain around his neck. From the chain dangled a small gold spoon. His shoes were yellow and appeared as if designed for a tap dancer. Rodney had come to Barringer five years previously. He had graduated from college and had joined the family-owned business in Detriville. After being in the business for a year, he found unexplainable financial transfers. He had carefully traced the transfers. He gathered each slip of related paperwork, checked on purchase requisitions, photographed related supplies, and carefully inventoried stated purchases. With growing suspicion, he documented cash flow to the activities of a cousin working in the business. He then traced his cousin's footsteps and activities. His developing case led to a warehouse that occupied his cousin at night.

At this point in his investigation he realized that a decision must be made to involve the police or to pursue the matter himself. He considered his options carefully. He could either take the sensible option of not involving himself in what was beginning to look like an illegal enterprise or he could live on a precipice. Like the occasional social aberrant, he decided that he liked top peak mountaineering.

The next day he invested heavily at a theatrical make-up shop. That evening an old man obviously drunk leaned against the side of the warehouse wall bordering an alley. The next morning the warehouse was found to have been broken into. Someone had obviously watched the preceding evening activities from an alleyway post, had watched the burglar alarm being set, had cut the wires, entered the building, and taken several bundles of goods. Panic ensued. Telephone calls were hastily made over lines that by then were monitored by appropriate law enforcement agencies. As panic mounted, an ill-considered attempt was made to evacuate the warehouse utilizing all available manpower. Captain Randolph Barringer was among those who participated in a midmorning raid, which resulted in the dismantling of a large narcotics operation triggered by an unknown informer. Later when all other agencies concentrated on the evidence to be presented in court, only Barringer retraced the discovery events backwards.

One morning he walked into Rodney Canthus's office. "Mr. Canthus, I am Captain Randolph Barringer of the Detriville Police Department. What you can trace, I can retrace. It was one of the best studied cases I have seen. If you enjoyed it as much as I think you did, then why not come work with me and do it every day?"

It is said that Canthus and the captain went out for lunch that day, and Canthus never went back to his business. He continued to live on the precipice concentrating only on narcotics. He was a will of the wisp living mostly at night, constantly in danger, stabbed and cut several times, shot once, and completely addicted to the peculiar excitement of being an unparalleled narcotics agent. He and Bartey were friends—each a loner at their own work but devoted companions when at leisure.

Ray Fielding was black sunshine. He has been born in Detriville as the oldest of six children. His father had left the family when Ray was twelve years old, and Ray felt both given responsibility and sensed the need to take it. He hit the streets taking any job available, most of which were overtly illegal or were open to serious question. He turned over to his mother and his siblings any money gained from these tasks, and his family was in no position to refuse it. He grew rapidly in statue and was of natural talent in weaving through the intricacies of street life. When he was eighteen, just short of graduating from high school, he was caught stealing from a parked car. His captor was a large black policeman who questioned him extensively before effecting an arrest. When they were through talking, the policeman said, "Ray, I'm gonna give you one chance. I'm gonna let you go because of your family. You quit the street, graduate from high school, join the service, and get a college education. You can do better that way for your Momma and brothers and sisters. If you keep this shit up, we gonna bust you and send you to prison and then what use are you? One condition. You write me after graduation and every six months after."

Ray was smart enough to understand. He got his college education and immediately joined the Detriville Police Force. He looked at Barringer and asked to be assigned to investigation.

Sergeant Ray Fielding was a big, easy going, amiable investigator who knew Detriville, both in the daytime and at night. He worked closely with Bartey and Canthus, and the three of them were an effective team.

# Chapter VI

February, 1974, was a cold month for the Detriville area. It rained frequently and was often cloudy. It was not an excellent year economically. The cold, the rise in energy costs, the bleakness, all led to a sense of despondency. People hoped that the spring would bring rejuvenation, but it was as yet several months away and February was dismal.

Albert Borgni drove toward his home on Pirates Beach on Tuesday, February 12, 1974. It was three-thirty in the afternoon. He had a severe headache. His abdomen hurt, and he had a feeling of constriction in his upper throat. Bills had mounted. The automobile was running in a furtive manner. Soon the motor would need repair, and he did not know if he could provide the cost. His wife and children were distant to him, as if they realized that something was amiss, and not amenable. He had no relationships at work, no friendships. Borgni had the feeling recently that he was a horse soldier in some ancient army and had gotten lost. His horse had died, and he had been left alone. His recent dejection had been replaced with anger. He disliked everyone.

He pulled the ailing car to a halt at the intersection of Pirates Beach Road and Canty Road and waited for the stop light to turn green. Across the intersection was the Pirates Beach Shopping Center. The car sputtered as the light turned green, and Borgni cursed. His anger invoked a need for something as yet undefined. Borgni interpreted the need as cigars, and as the old automobile coughed and sputtered across the intersection, he turned into the shopping center. He stopped at the drug store and went inside and bought three cigars. As he paid for the cigars at the cash register, the clerk smiled at him and said, "Bad for your health." Borgni looked at her with intense hatred. She looked back curiously, wondering at the obvious hostility.

Borgni walked to his car while unwrapping one of the cigars. He opened the door, slid into the drivers seat, and started to turn the ignition key.

Twenty-five yards away, Carrie Ballard passed on her way home from school. She held several school books in her right arm with the left hand crossed to help support the load. Her mind was occupied with the events of the day. Larry had asked her to go with him to the basketball game on the coming Friday night. She was happy and content. She felt that she was winning, socially, scholastically and pridefully. She was happy with herself and, therefore, happy with the world. Carrie was fourteen. She was the only daughter of devoted parents, and the world was at a rosy peak at this moment.

Borgni's hand closed around the half opened cigar. It felt like a knife handle, and he felt the distinct urge to thrust a knife into the girl walking away from him. As he watched, he was engrossed with the urge to imprison her, to bind her, to have total control over her. Seized with visions of a young girl bound in ropes and contorted into unusual positions, Borgni bolted from his car back into the shopping center. He wanted a knife, and with his mind racing he ran towards the Red and Blue grocery store. He went immediately to the utility counter, and quickly selected a small, sharp paring knife. He hurried to the checkout counter, paid, thrust the knife into his coat and left.

As he approached the sidewalk, he saw the girl turn onto a side road that coursed through a wooded area toward a housing development. He hurried after the girl.

Carrie suddenly realized that someone was rapidly approaching her. As she turned to look behind, Borgni's left hand caught her hair and his right hand thrust the knife at her throat.

"Come with me, little girl."

Carrie dropped her books.

"Pick them up and walk into there. I've just robbed a store, and you're my hostage. Be quiet or I'll cut your throat."

Borgni pushed her roughly into the woods. He stopped her at a small oak tree. They were now out of sight of the road.

"Mister, please don't hurt me. I've got to get home. My mother is waiting for me." Carrie began to sob.

"Shut up. Kneel down there by that tree. Stop that crying."

Borgni was looking intently at Carrie. She was a perfect catch, young, terrified, crying. She huddled at the base of the tree, a crumpled human being, filled with fear. It was the kind of fear that keeps the mind from functioning, and makes it wallow in the waste of useless dread. Carrie cowered in fear, not really concerned with her eventual fate, but focused on wishing that the evil man standing beside her was not there.

"I'm going to have to tie you up with your clothes. Stand up and take off all your clothes except your panties. You can keep your bra on, too."

Carrie stood hesitantly. She was shaking badly. The morning had been comfortable an hour previously, but she now felt distinctly chilled. She hesitated and looked sadly at Borgni, a look much like that of a hurt puppy, afraid and dejected.

Borgni's left hand shot out grasping Carrie's hair. Brutally he lifted her against the tree. His right hand, still containing the knife came up beneath her chin.

"If you don't do what I want you to, I'll slit your goddamned throat." His voice had changed from its usual softness to a harsh almost militaristic manner. His eyes were jet black now, fierce, belligerent. They were like the eyes of a hawk, aggressive, ready to attack. His body leaned forward and Carrie could feel his breath, not just hear it or count it, but feel it as a tangible cloud of pure anger. She essentially collapsed. Her legs buckled, her arms fell by her sides, lifeless. As her strength ebbed, Borgni let her slump into a semi-squatting position beside the tree. He reached over her and grasped the back of her sweater and drew it slowly over her head and off of her arms. She provided no resistance, barely lifting her arms to free the sleeves. Her head bent forward, her eyes gazed in an unfocused manner on the ground in front of her. Borgni looked at her carefully and instinctively realized her incapacity. He reached down and placing his finger beneath her chin lifted her head backward. She maintained the posture that he placed her in and did not move as he began unbuttoning her blouse. Her gaze was now into the woods but was listless and unseeing. She did not tremble now and did not move at all. He pulled the blouse backwards from her shoulders and arms. As the blouse was freed from her wrists, the arms swung downward again, of their own accord and not in concert with any physical capacity.

"Stand up."

She tried and simply could not stand. He lifted her and essentially propped her against the tree. He undid her skirt and let it fall to the ground around her ankles. She was now clad in her bra and panty hose. Continuing to realize her weakness, he pushed the panty hose downward.

"Raise your knee."

She did as he directed.

"Raise the other one."

Borgni stripped away the panty hose and then, quite within her vision, began cutting it into strips. As he thrust the knife blade violently through the crotch of the panty hose and ripped it upward, she shuddered, her only recent movement.

When he had completed the sectioning of the strips he turned her toward the tree and bound her wrists behind her, slowly, meticulously, making each knot in a fashion as if prescribed by a recipe. His attention was focused on the knot itself, the way in which it was tied rather than its purpose of securely binding her. As he overlapped and intertwined the bindings it was as if he were caught in a ritual of bondage rather than a rite of human destruction. He next wadded a piece, and as he pushed it into her mouth, her eyes opened widely in terror. Her body came alive and tensed as if to determine the direction in which to run. Borgni, the ever present hawk, sensed her tension and quickly again gained control. Grasping her again by the hair, he pressed her firmly against the tree.

"You move, and I'll stick this knife in your ass."

Again her muscles sagged, and she leaned against the tree. He bound the gag in place with a strip around her mouth and neck.

Borgni stepped backward to view his handiwork. Her wrists were crossed behind her and bound evenly. Her right shoulder leaned against the tree. Her feet were slightly apart but she held her knees together in an almost expectant manner. Borgni circled her, the cat with the mouse. He carefully inspected her nearly naked physique and was content with the degree that fear held her immobile.

Satisfied with her bondage and fear, he approached her from behind. He stood closely behind her and began moving his hands across her shoulders onto her chest beneath her bra. He would then turn her, pressing her against the tree with his body, applying pressure to produce compression and fear. He pressed against her left side and slid his left hand into the front of her panties and his right hand down between her buttocks. Each movement was deliberate, seemingly more designed to produce an effect in her than in himself. He remained fairly calm, extremely intent, but not in an excited manner, his intenseness and the constant pressure all but pressed the very life from Carrie. As both hands would simultaneously invade her body's most sensitive area, her conscious mind would explode with the combination of stimulation and terror. These effects were visible, and it was the physical appearance of her desperation that held Borgni's attention.

After extensive pressure and movement with his hands and body, he would turn her toward the tree and walk away a few steps to simply look at her. He turned her, bent her over, made her kneel, placed her on her back and forced her to assume an infinite variety of positions. They had been in the woods about a half hour. A car passed slowly, quite audible and near, but its physical presence was hidden by the dense undergrowth of the wooded area. The car brought Borgni back to reality. The girl had mentioned that her mother was waiting. Possibly the car represented the mother searching for her daughter. The thought of a larger woman confronting him bothered Borgni.

"Stand back up. I'm going to tie you to this tree. Turn around."

Borgni turned her to face away from the tree. He placed a strip of panty hose around her neck and the tree. He pulled tightly, visibly choking her. The length of the strip only allowed the tying of one knot. The bulk of the strip distributed itself so evenly across her neck that it did not apply as a choking ligature. The car drove by again. Borgni decided to leave. He could not deny the presence of the automobile and could not focus his entire attention on the girl. He was becoming confused. The girl was not offering any resistance, the strip could not be drawn tighter, the car might return.

Borgni left.

# Chapter VII

Carrie Ballard freed herself, hastily put on her blouse and shorts and ran home. Her mother called the Detriville police, and Detective Bartey was dispensed to investigate. Bartey reported to Barringer and the team that afternoon.

"What happened, Bob?" Barringer said.

Bartey pulled his notebook and began.

"Patrol took the call. They called me right after they talked to the girl's mother. They patrolled the area, but didn't come up with anything. When I got there, the mother was pretty upset. She had called the father who came home quickly after I got there. He kinda lost his cool but settled down after a bit."

Barringer mused. Most of the people who got upset with Bartey cooled down pretty quickly. When Bartey wished, he was almost imperturbable. His quiet intensity apparently caused people to begin to think rather than to become more emotionally disturbed. Additionally, when confronted, Bartey had the habit of getting rid of whatever might be in his hands, dropped his arms to his side, and apparently relaxed and squarely faced the confrontation. While his posture was not that of belligerence at these times, it did somehow convey physical confidence. Barringer wondered if it were not some sort of primeval body language that said, "Watch out, I'm ready." Barringer's thoughts passed quickly as Bartey continued.

"When the father had calmed down, I persuaded him and Carrie to accompany me to the scene of the attack. We walked through every step that Carrie took after she left the bus. The way I see it, the attacker was in the shopping center, saw her get off the bus, followed her down the highway to Blanding, and then walked up behind her. The trouble is, the timing didn't match. When we walked through it, I caught up with her long before she got to Blanding Street even if I walked slowly. Something delayed the attacker. When Carrie described the knife it hit me that it was odd to carry one like that in your pocket, and the light dawned that maybe the dude bought the knife in the shopping center. That would have accounted for the delay. Sure enough, in the supermarket there are some small green handled kitchen knives. I bought one and showed it to Carrie. She stated that it was exactly the same kind used on her." Bartey reached into his box of note pads and produced a small green handled plastic paring knife.

Bartey continued. "I got Crime Scene to come out and go over the assault site. The guy apparently moved around a lot. Carrie said that he would make her assume a position and then go stand first in one place for a while and then go to another, apparently just to get a different view. The foot tracks seemed to corroborate this. She said he didn't say much, but seemed to be enjoying the position of being overpowering. He would place her in a new position, fondle her some, would be breathing pretty hard at times, but seemed to be content with just watching her or at least just scaring her. Carrie says the guy was about my size, dark complexioned, black hair, dark mustache, and extremely dangerous looking. When I asked her about the dangerous bit, she said he just scared her to death, something about his eyes, the way he would look at her."

"Bartey, her description of the assailant's age is younger than the girls missing last year on Pirates Beach?"

"Yes, sir."

"Captain," Bartey said, "Why do you reckon this guy didn't kill Carrie?"

Barringer considered the question for a moment. First, it was rare for Bartey to ask such a question in front of others, and secondly, he seemed genuinely perplexed that Carrie had not been killed. Possibly Bartey's mind didn't deal with human inconsistency very well. To Bartey an animal was an animal and should be viewed and treated as such. Maybe the reason for Bartey's successes were his directness of thought and his lack of appreciation of undue complexity.

"I don't know, Bob. Maybe we're dealing with a weird kind of psycho who gets his jollies from scaring young girls. Maybe killing them is not in his plan or maybe he doesn't even have a plan. If your theory about the knife is correct, maybe he wasn't intentionally waiting for her, but just happened to see her get off the bus. Maybe something then went berserk in his head. I don't know. Now, suppose he didn't have a plan and was just in the shopping center. Why was he there?"

"I considered that, Captain. Carrie's father and I took her back to the school bus stop. I parked in various locations in the parking lot that would give opportunity to see her when she got off the bus. It gave me a pretty good idea where the dude had parked if it happened that way. When I figured that out, I looked at the stores that he might have gone to. The drug store was likely. I interviewed the girl that was on the cash register that afternoon.

"She remembered a guy like Carrie described, and she remembered that he acted kind of peculiar."

"In what way?"

"She said he acted angry."

"Did you talk to the clerks in the grocery store?"

"Yes, sir, but none of them remembered anybody buying a knife."

"Anything else?"

"No, sir, that's about it—except, maybe one thing."

"What's that?"

"This dude scared the hell out of Carrie. I've checked back with her. She's still afraid. There's something bad wrong with this guy. We need to nail him."

There was a general stir among the men. All agreed with Bartey. They all recognized that they were dealing with a contagious sickness. If not contained, it would inevitably contaminate others. Their driving force was containment. It had been trained into them since they were rookies and when the opportunity to contain a lethal sickness happened, it brought them to a restless state. Despite their intensity, further investigation yielded no clues as to the identity of the assailant.

# Chapter VIII

Mid February 1974 began with a beautiful morning. There were no clouds and a fresh breeze energized the surf to pound the sand of Pirates Beach, an exercise that had been repeated daily for several thousand years. On the sea islands, the surf's increasing confrontation with the beach is more than a repetitive monotony. To a puppy, or a child, the surf is a constant challenge, a vulnerable opponent capable of being smashed into a million shiny salt water droplets. To lovers, the surf is a permissive companion, allowing an opportunity for being in each others arms, permitting love under a watchful but never seeing eye. To runners it is a reason for running; to the excited it is a calming influence; to the reflective it is steadiness. To the hunter lost in the thick palmettos, the surf is a direction by which to find the beach. To the hunted, the surf is the direction from which to flee into the thickets.

To Albert Borgni, the surf may have been an disorganizing force. Mood, be it the height of mania, or the low of gray depression, occasionally interrupts the usual organization of biological clocks, and it is possible that the surf affected Albert Borgni. If his genetic code was born and nurtured on the steppes of Asia, or in the deserts of Babylon, or elsewhere, and was then transported in a relatively rapid manner to a spot physically and audibly attuned to the beating surf, then perhaps a disorganization resulted. It is difficult, and perhaps wasteful, to express how deeply and by what mechanism the brain of Albert Borgni became affected, but by whatever responsible mechanism, it was an undeniable and lasting one, one so completely beyond control that he did not even bother to resist.

Borgni woke and struggled for the front doorway. He picked up a cigar and a pack of matches from a nearby table and stumbled onto the front porch. He felt exhausted, as if he had not slept at all, and yet he did not feel physically tired. There was a vague energy stirring within him, and as he sat, he barely realized that something was astir within him. The feeling lasted only a second. He lit the cigar.

Borgni listened to the sound of the surf. His house was on the second row from the beach. While he could not see the surf, its low incessant pounding was easily audible.

The surf at Pirates Beach had a unique quality. Perhaps the sound, properly analyzed by spectrographic techniques in some highly sophisticated laboratory, would only reveal amplitudes, pitches, and resonance characteristic of surf anywhere. Perhaps it would not. It is at least possible that the shape of a beach, its latitude and longitude, its relation to time and tide, and the actual physical characteristics of sand, clay, marl, and shell, all combine for an individual sound. Whatever it is, the combination of the sound of the Pirates Beach surf, the physical presence of that particular morning, and the unrest of the night, produced a barely perceptible, but ominous feeling in Albert Borgni's body.

The cigar tasted murky but vaguely pleasant. He did not actually notice the pleasure, but his body realized it and settled in the chair. Borgni did not think well. His mind rumbled around, bumbling, bouncing off each object brought to it by his senses, but never really stopping to encompass one object. His mind did not hold an object long enough to examine details and consider them, compare one to another, and marvel at each. Only occasionally, rarely, unpredictably, did his mind suspend its random activities to focus on one set of senses. This morning it was gradually beginning to lay a framework for one of those rare occasions. Perhaps it was the restless night, perhaps the surf, perhaps all these things put together, perhaps chance itself. Whatever the reason, the mental circuits began their peculiar pattern. Switches began to close, a pattern began to form, and the abnormal center in the brain began to be disturbed.

Borgni felt uneasy and restless. The cigar had not helped, and he was out of others. He must go downtown and get some more, and perhaps a paper or a magazine, or something. He frowned. He was restless. Something was wrong and he did not understand exactly what. He was not hungry. He thought for a moment of walking on the beach but quickly discarded the thought. There was nothing to do, nowhere to go, no drive, no ambition, no ability, no nothing. He had a growing anger.

Borgni went back to bed. It was all he could do. As he slid into bed he glanced at his wife and realized how much he hated her. He closed his eyes tightly, desperately trying to go back to sleep, realizing vaguely what was slowly but inexorably building up within him. For a fleeting second, an instant, as if someone had projected a quick photograph on a screen, he saw a mental image. The mental image was a picture, stark, devoid of background, but clear, almost as if someone had produced reality. The picture was a young girl, a teenager, perhaps twelve or thirteen years of age. She was clothed only in white panties. Her skin was very white. She was on her knees. Her ankles were bound together with a white cloth. Her wrists were bound behind her back, and a white rope extended from her ankles to her wrists and from there to her neck. The rope was fairly tight and it had her head slightly twisted to the left, the face to the left, the right cheek down, her relatively long, auburn hair to the right. Her shoulders were down as if compressed by some weight larger than her own, or was it the way she was bound? Her face was rather plain, not remarkable except for the expression. It was clear that the child was in significant pain.

Borgni slept soundly until early afternoon. He did not stir when his wife arose earlier. He did not smell the pleasantness of breakfast. He did not hear the chatter of the children. He slept restfully. His body relaxed, almost as if it knew it was preparing for something. His mind was totally devoid of any further images. It had changed from its normal state of chaotic meandering. Circuits had begun to form a mental receptiveness. Whatever the senses would bring into this mental area would be met with a different format than usually existed. Albert Borgni's mind had reverted to some dark, distant, primeval trap. It wanted something. It was armed and dangerous.

Borgni awoke at 1:30 p.m. He arose, shaved, and showered quickly. Dried, he paid particular attention to his appearance. He fished in the medicine cabinet and found a small vial of aftershave lotion. He carefully applied a small amount and paused, sniffing himself. Next he combed his thick, dark hair and adjusted his mustache. He dressed studiously, selecting the dark trousers from the right hand part of the closet. He pulled on long black socks, first the left and then the right one above the round scar on his lower right leg. He looked at the scar, vaguely remembering. A white tee shirt and a soft white favorite blouse completed the clothes. He slid a wide, black leather belt into place and then stepped into the black boots with the pointed toes. The boots were special, the leather was relatively soft above the ankles but firm below, the soles plain but thick, the heels high and constructed of hard rubber. The boots tightened with well constructed zippers. He wore no watch or jewelry. He carried only a wallet and handkerchief, and despite the occasional need, he had no pocket knife.

Borgni was ready. It was nearly two o'clock. The family had gone somewhere. Elaine's books were on the breakfast table. William's toy plastic gun was on the sofa. There was cereal on the table but Borgni was not hungry. He remembered he was out of cigars. He erroneously misidentified an inner feeling as wanting a cigar and he made the decision to go downtown and buy some, and maybe a paper.

As usual the car was difficult to start, a situation which always angered Albert. In a perturbed mood he drove without event for nine blocks to the downtown area. He turned left onto Main Street and stopped in an easily accessible parking lot in the front of the Pirates Beach Drug Store. He opened the door of the car and stepped onto the curb before noticing a group across the street in front of the restaurant. In front of the restaurant stood three happy, talkative, teenage girls, one standing on the sidewalk and the other two standing beside the curb. The girl on the sidewalk was the most lively. She was slender, well tanned, and athletic in appearance. She wore a blue blouse and dark blue sweater and jeans. Her hair was auburn and as she tossed her head with the conversation, one could sense a self-confidence and capability. At the moment she was addressing a slightly smaller blonde girl on her right who giggled and bubbled with every phrase. This girl was dressed neatly but loosely in an informal way. She personified good nature and pleasantness. The third girl was different from the other two. She had her back to Borgni, but it was easily seen that she was slightly taller than her bubbly companions. She had long brown hair, and stood quietly while other two talked. She had on a white blouse that contrasted with the dark hair falling on its collar and on her shoulders. She wore a neat tan sweater, a brown skirt, white socks and oxford shoes. As she occasionally turned, her face appeared attractive but not unusually arresting. She smiled but did not compete with the other two in the liveliness of their conversation. The characteristics that set her as different from the other two were that she appeared to be more feminine. Mary Brady was feminine but not obvious as such. She appeared to be budding but not yet blooming, vulnerable, a wounded rabbit.

Borgni had barely put his foot upon the curb when he noted the three girls. He summed up the entire scene in less than a few seconds. His chest and abdomen tightened. He realized that he was again caught in the circumstances of his peculiar morbidity. He climbed back in the car and watched, safe from suspicion, letting his inner, bizarre, genetically transmitted behavioral code envelop him. The feeling was like an electronic computer that is programmed to perform simple daily tasks and suddenly receives a new set of instructions. New tape drives turn, new lights begin to blink and glimmer, a new motor begins to hum. The printer begins to turn. The computer is being transformed into an entirely different function, and in this instance an ominous one. This is not the first time; the symptoms were too well known to Borgni, and for a second he resisted, knowing intuitively what would likely happen. The initial hesitation was only momentary, for after the first hesitant moment, his loss of self control, the rest began to happen quickly. Borgni stared intensely at the three girls. His mind was by no means decided, but it had already begun to focus on Mary Brady. When she turned her head so the face was apparent, Borgni could imagine the face engrossed with pain. When she turned her body slightly, Borgni could mentally make her blouse and sweater disappear. He could almost imagine touching her, controlling her, providing fear and supplication. He jarred himself from his fantasy. He knew that this particular opportunity had been building for some time and would not diminish. He knew that he had to get prepared. He did not even consider whether he would involve all of the girls or just one. He only knew that he had to go back to the house and obtain the instruments that would allow him the only satisfaction of his life, the domination of the young, helpless, or stricken female body.

He started the car and drove rapidly back to the house. Without a thought he strode through the front door, picked up his son's toy pistol, put a small kitchen paring knife in his jacket pocket and went out the back door, down the steps, into the backyard. He strode to the clothesline and rapidly cut a few sections of the clothesline into approximately three foot lengths. He folded these and placed them in his left jacket pocket. He went back through the house dropping the knife on the kitchen table. He disliked knives and mistrusted them. Only occasionally had he resorted to a knife, and then only out of necessity.

Finally, he paused, thought for a moment and returned to his bedroom closet. He reached high onto the top shelf, found a section of a broom handle, thrust it into his back pocket, and walked hastily out of the house. Back in the car, he drove more quickly to town, and again turned the corner. As he turned, Mary was in the street, saying something final to the other two. Clearly the group was parting and Mary apparently was going somewhere by herself. Borgni flushed. His feeling of wanting something intensified. The hunt was on, and the hunter was no longer under his own control.

He drove beyond the parting girls and carefully parked in a safe, unobtrusive spot on Main Street. He glanced into his rear view mirror and noted that Mary was now crossing the street directly behind him. He even noted that she glanced in his direction, but there was no recognition of importance in her glance. She began walking down Adams Street going east in the direction of Borgni's house.

Borgni stepped out of the car and crossed the parking lot. He followed Mary who ambled leisurely on about fifty yards away, but out of sight behind a row of buildings on Adams Street. Borgni reached First Street before Mary did but hesitated until she crossed the intersection. He watched her cross and noted the carefree, innocent, almost careless stride of her walk. She appeared totally absorbed in her thoughts. Her vulnerability was now outstanding. There was no one else on the street and Borgni's thoughts did not include the people in the nearby houses. He was a hawk entirely intent on his prey with no thought or regard for anything else. Some part of his mind saw all of his surroundings and listened for cars, glanced around for police or protectors, but did so in a totally automatic mode.

Borgni began his approach, crossing the intersection and only about fifty feet behind Mary. Now he intently surveyed the scene, this time not automatically, but studiously, like the scout of Ghengis Khan a thousand years ago.

Borgni had not broken his stride, and assured that the surroundings did not threaten him, he quickened his pace. Just as Mary heard his steps, he caught her right arm with his left hand and thrust the toy pistol into her right side.

"Come with me, little girl."

The rabbit was paralyzed. She could see the gun and had no reason to believe it was not real. But it was not the gun that almost arrested her heart. Mary Brady saw a soldier, a menacing, dangerous man, an animal, a beast, something that did not even belong on Pirates Beach, something she had never seen before, even in the movies. Her perception came almost from his eyes, but it was more than that. It was his whole being, his malice, the intentness, the overpowering obviousness that he was in control. His control was the production of fear, and she was immensely afraid.

"I just robbed a bar and shot the owner. You are my hostage. Walk with me and you won't be hurt. Run or scream and I will kill you."

She did not test the words. She did not consider the meaning, much less the veracity. She was caught. There was no resistance. This foreign soldier controlled her.

She walked, half led, between the next two houses on the beach. They turned east in the direction of Borgni's house. He knew where he was taking her, having been there before. His thoughts were not on previous occasions, molestations, struggles, or bodies, but entirely immersed in a relation with this girl. As his hand firmly but not severely held her arm, he knew that this was his best catch so far. He had already glanced at her acutely. Seeing her the hair was perfect, long, well groomed, but capable of breaking about or being blown to her face in a provocative fashion. Her face was not beautiful, but was pretty. The features had entirely collapsed but he knew how to rejuvenate them. The neck was long and he could not look at it without seeing a knotted rope. The blouse and sweater would disappear revealing breasts, small and pointed, but present, which would receive his attention. Her body appeared supple, and he noted that he would test how much. Her ankles were trim, and again, he saw ropes tied about them.

They were walking east on the beach. Despite the fact that she walked as an automaton, lifeless, with head and eyes straight and arms relatively motionless by her sides, and his hand still holding her arm, they did not appear unnatural. Only once did she look up and then only for a second glancing in the direction of her house, but knowing that her parents were not there, then she looked down again dejectedly. She knew what was happening and knew or believed that she could not do anything about it. They walked eastward at a steady pace.

There was little conversation. He had what he wanted, and was satisfied with the ease and completeness of it. There was no reason for anyone to interfere with them on the beach and no one was present. It was distinctly cool but not painfully cold.

She was despondent, too young to know what to do and just old enough to know that what she saw and feared in his eyes was ominous. It meant to her that she was going to suffer, suffer in a despicable and debasing way. It was a feeling of dirty hopelessness. She was caught, and the life had gone out of her as if burned out by a lightning bolt of fear. Now she was dejected by her helplessness, trudging numbly, not thinking, devoid of energy to think, cry, or do anything but walk along beaten by fear.

Borgni saw the house ahead. There was a boardwalk to the beach, but he took a shortcut across the dunes. The next few houses appeared empty as were many at this time of year. As they crossed the dunes, a few thoughts struggled towards the surface of Borgni's mind, but were not strong enough to swim the tides that were churning in the turmoil of its present consciousness. These thoughts turned and were lost back into a deep, hideous memory. They concerned what lay beneath the sandy dunes near this house.

Borgni pushed the front side door of 904 Adams Street inward. It was locked, but the door, and subsequently the lock, did not fit and could easily be forced inward. They entered a front living room. The house contained this room, an adjoining bedroom, a bathroom, and a kitchenette/dining room combination. Outside there was a shower stall to wash the salt and sand away before entering the house. Toward the top of the shower stall were two copper pipes. From the pipes hung two strips of cloth. The hung as if they missed a part of them that had been cut away.

Borgni pushed Mary onto a flat couch in one corner of the living room.

She virtually collapsed, putting her head down, closing her eyes. She was partially lying on her left side with her feet still on the floor. Borgni pulled up a chair and sat watching her as she rubbed her right arm.

"I am going to tie you up. Turn onto your stomach and put your hands behind your back."

As she did so, she began to awaken from her stupor. The reality of being touched again, if being bound, frightened her into reality.

"Please don't hurt me, please let me go home, please don't tie me up, please, please, please." Her voice was pathetic, a whimper. She turned her head so as not to look at the frightening animal that had now begun to bind her wrists behind her back. He finished and stood to survey its completion. He now let his eyes roam the entirety of her back. Her hair had fallen across her face, obscuring most of it, but he could see her right eye, which was open and wide with fear. He reached down and pulled her hair aside, and she tightly closed her eyes. He walked to the foot of the couch and removed both her shoes and socks, and bound her ankles with another piece of the clothesline. He then lifted her skirt with his right hand, and slid his left hand upward along the back of her thighs to her buttocks. Despite her pressing her knees together, he slid his hand between her upper thighs onto the entrance of her vagina. She began whimpering. Borgni withdrew his hand and reached down and grasped a part of the bedspread that covered the couch. He tore several pieces. He thrust one portion into her mouth and tied another around her face and neck so as to provide an effective gag. He then sat down.

Once, a long time ago, a little boy had caught a frog. He had tied a string from one leg to a stick, then another string to the other leg and a stick, he then staked the frog over a small ant hill. Time and again he would re-do the tying, and the staking, and occasionally inflict a small injury. The boy sat for hours mesmerized with the frog's helplessness and futility and progressive weakness.

So sat Borgni. He simply watched. There is as yet no capability of describing Borgni's emotions at this time. He was not satisfied or sexually satiated, nor was he really stimulated. He was not curious or elated or excited. He simply watched. He was like the little boy with the frog. He was hypnotized. He had produced what he wanted. Nothing was present to interfere. He had allowed his mind to ingest the helpless little girl bound before it, and his mind responded. In hypnosis, a curtain closes. It is a silent curtain. It is as if the curtain is constructed of a soft flannel type of heavy cloth, dark and sound absorbing. It is hung on silent invisible runners. Ordinarily it is open, retracted, permitting all the light and sound of the outside world into the mind, and the mind is alive, vibrant and busy like a factory, managing the business of the outside world. But now the curtain had closed, silently, and nothing was permitted except a small, constricted opening near the top between the curtains. Inside, the mind was still, attentive, but motionless, absorbing the bound child.

After a fairly lengthy period, perhaps thirty to forty minutes, a biological clock began an arousal process. First the mind began to move again, and then the curtains opened slowly and retracted.

Borgni spoke. "I am going to untie your hands and feet. I want you to take off all your clothes. You can keep your panties on. I am not going to hurt you, but I must tie you back up."

Mary was numb. She was essentially paralyzed. She had been flying in a happy pattern, gay and carefree, zooming and swooping, and floating gently in the air. Suddenly, without any warning, as if in the most horrible of nightmares, she had flown directly into a giant spider web and was imprisoned. As she opened her eyes, she looked directly into the awesome face of the world's largest and most hideous of black, hairy, spiders. She knew she was to be hurt, but there was absolutely nothing she could do. Her energy had been drained away. As if in a nightmare, she could not move.

Her hands and feet were unbound. She sat up on the edge of the couch, her head bowed. She slowly unbuttoned her sweater and like an automaton, removed it and placed it beside her. She unbuttoned her blouse and slipped it off, showing a bra that was not really necessary, but a matter of pride. She dully unhitched the bra and let it slip onto her blouse. Her head had sunk lower, the undressing of her dignity, and now it was gone and nothing was left. As if she knew what to do, like an older woman, she unsnapped her skirt and shifted her weight to slip it down and off, slowly placing it beside her. She was devastated, empty, desolate; her shoulders sagged as if broken and she closed her eyes, beaten.

Borgni watched. His mind began to stir, to once again imagine, to invent, to fantasize. He saw the ropes, and they again began to awaken a sensation in him. The sensation was a peculiar one, not lust, not simple sensuality, but rather a complex feeling with sex just barely attached to it. His body and mind now interlocked for the inevitable. They were locked in a sense of domination, his entire being now wanting to dominate. Mixed, in a pathological sense, was a sexual urge, but it was so suppressed and intertwined in the confusion of the more primitive urges that it was lost to his need to overpower.

Borgni retied Mary's wrists behind her back. She offered no resistance. Standing at her left side, he lifted the bound wrists with his right hand. She necessarily leaned forward. With his left hand he grasped her right breast and massaged it allowing his left wrist and arm to rub against her left breast. Her face was immobile, her eyes open, dull, defeated. He then ran his left hand down into the front of her panties, but did not actually enter her. He then switched hands and explored her buttocks with his right hand.

"Get on the couch, little girl." She crawled onto the couch, her hands bound behind her. He separated her legs and again explored her buttocks and perineum with his hand, this time outside of her panties. He paused, extracted the broom handle from his pocket and sat, looking at it for a few minutes. He then held it in his right hand, and with his left, spread her buttocks. He applied the instrument to the anal region, pushing, but not forcing, her panties partially into the external portion of her anus. When he would do so, he would pause and look at the indentation, then straightened it out, and began again. After repeating this ritual innumerable times at a dozen different angles, he paused. He readjusted the stick in his hand, this time firmly. He tensed, took a deep breath and thrust with all of his strength. The child straightened with pain, screamed into her gag and literally convulsed with agony and despair.

He rolled her onto her side so that she faced him and the room. He sat down again and stared at her. She was now only a limp naked rag of a child. His eyes traveled her entire body as if memorizing it or simply dwelling on it as the sole purpose for all of his actions.

He rolled her over onto her other side and stood, again, staring.

He turned her onto her abdomen and as he purposefully turned her head to the wall, he tied her ankles.

He sat for a long time. Both were silent. There was no life in the room. There was no anguish, no pity, no vibrancy, nothing human. Both were quiet. Finally, a switch closed in Borgni's mind. A circuit began. Thoughts began which had laid dormant all this time, but were as much a part of the day as the pounding of the surf.

Borgni picked up a piece of rope and tied it loosely around Mary's neck. He ran the other end around the bindings of her ankles. Standing at the foot of the couch, he pulled. Her head came up off the couch. Her feet were pulled upward toward her head. Her back arched. He tied a knot. Her eyes opened, stark with terror. Her muscles tensed automatically increasing the tightness of the rope. She was alive now, aware, knowledgeable of horror, struggling, but bound, and bound in such a way that none of her muscles could act against anything but the rope, and then with no mechanical advantage. The light was fading, the nightmare was abating, the heart, having raced, was running out of oxygen and no more was coming. The heart was faltering.

She relaxed, and never moved again.

Borgni had been standing. He now sat down again. Now he was wet with perspiration. He sat and stared. After a while, he reached over and pushed her onto her side.

Slowly, like the rising of the moon, his mind began to assimilate reality. Slowly, his body became noticeable to him and he stirred in a barely perceptible way in his chair. Very slowly, he became aware that he had killed another young girl.

Borgni felt slightly ill. He began to perceive the sensation of panic, the need to run. He repressed these feelings. He knew he must hide what he had done. He walked quickly to his house, got a shovel and walked back to where a half naked innocent young girl lay contorted in ropes on a dirty couch in an empty house.

He walked to the end of the boardwalk in front of the house and began digging a shallow grave. He glanced up and down the beach. It was a grey day and seemed to be getting colder. The wind blew sand into the grave while he was digging. He shoveled quickly. A sense of panic was building, but there was no scaffold for it to build upon. He was emotionally exhausted, empty, divest of any further feeling, overcome, turned inside-out. He hurried into the house, undid the rope at the neck and carried the dead child onto the cold forbidding beach. Again, he looked onto the beach and found it empty. He walked to the grave and dropped the child into it. The rope remained attached to her ankles. She fell head first, her face in the cold wet sand, her hair covering her face, her hands still bound. Her legs were straight, one hand partially cocked up, but he did not bother to compress it. He returned to the house, gathered her clothes, returned and threw them into the grave. He hastily covered the body and clothes with sand. Her upturned hand was buried, but only superficially.

The beach was silent. The waves were not making any noticeable sound. A peculiar chill could be felt. Albert Borgni returned home.

# Chapter IX

Eugene Wilson lived at Pirates Beach on a precipice. It was not a physical precipice for there are none at Pirates Beach. The island is flat except for the dunes. Gene Wilson's precipice was an emotional one.

He was born thirty-five years previously on a small farm in the middle of the state. His father was a farmer, solid and dependable. His mother was adorable. She was small, delicate, very pretty and effervescent. She was good humor and pleasantness personified. The parents of Gene Wilson were devoted to each other in a quiet sort of way. Gene never saw his father touch his mother in a personal way, but frequently watched his mother flitter around his father, stirring his coffee, rearranging a pillow, kissing him lightly on the cheek. He had been the only child and was, therefore, even more focused on his parent's interaction than if he had brothers or sisters with whom to share and divert attention and energies. With the constraint of the relatively lonely life of the farm and the quiet attitude of his father, Gene's emotions had converged upon his mother. She was the sunshine, the bright cheerfulness of the daylight, the lightness of laughter and good nature. She was the softness of night, the sweetness of summer evenings, the companion during storms. Gene Wilson adored his mother. He grew up discussing everything with her. She taught him to read and to love the process of learning. Not intellectual herself, she appreciated his introspection and she supported his mental exercise. The father was not well-educated, but the house contained excellent books and magazines. They appeared as if by magic and were consumed by the boy. The mother delighted in having her son read and recite the adventures and stories that literature spills upon an eager mind.

The mother was a frilly, energetic, ever busy, joyful china doll. She was a good cook and a good homemaker. The boy's clothes were always clean and neat, meals were hot, and conversation was pleasant and lively.

The father was a quiet, pensive man. He struggled with the farm, frequently working to exhaustion. He ate his supper quietly and retired early, and was up at first light and gone upon another natural task. He was never unpleasant, but one instinctively knew to leave him alone when he was tired or brooding at the frequent burdens imposed by being caught between the hard tasks of nature and the profiteering businessmen of the city. He provided as well as his talents and energies allowed.

When the boy was thirteen, he began to realize that the world was larger than his farm and family and the small school in the city. He was still totally dependent on his mother and continued his adoration, but he was beginning to listen to others also. It is the most difficult phase of life. He was beginning to carefully shed the cocoon, or at least, to unwrap part of it.

A farm, because it is a living thing, a semi-autonomous entity, struggling against the hard and capricious winds of nature, is never consistent, and the spring had gone badly for the farm. Virtually no rain had fallen and one crop after another failed. In desperation, like a gambler following his instincts, the father made a decision to risk heavily on a big money crop. Surely rain would come, but it didn't. The family was in significant debt, and the father was exhausted and depressed, wandering about, brooding. The mother took unintentional refuge at the church, helping with meetings, decorating and fundraising. In the early fall, the mother had a mid-week church meeting. She left after supper, as she walked across the porch where the boy was reading and the father sat pensively, she glanced at the darkening sky.

"It almost feels like rain, and there are some clouds over there, just beyond the trees."

The father looked up, studiously. He said nothing, and the mother left, promising to be back early.

The boy was in his room reading when his mother returned. He realized it was later than usual and, in fact, that it was beyond his bedtime. He heard his mother on the porch and realized from the sound of the car engine that it was not the family car. He heard his father say something rude to a man who had apparently brought his mother home. He heard a car drive off. He later explained that he vaguely remembered his mother protesting, saying something to the effect that everything was all right, that someone just did not understand. There was an explosion, then another. He did not remember much after that. He remembered seeing his mother's hand, tiny and delicate, and blood. They told him later that he had made a telephone call, explaining carefully that his father had shot his mother and then himself.

Gene Wilson had been further raised by his uncle and aunt, his mother's sister. It was a calm, uneventful home in the city.

He did not allow himself to remember the country and strenuously repressed his memories of his mother, for he simply could not endure the pain. The financial situation of his uncle's small store did not allow college. He joined the army as an only alternative, and endured the physical deprivation of the service stoically. His relaxation was in his books. The others left him alone, realizing that he was different. He performed as well as the others, but had no more initiative than was expected, detesting war and violence. He saw death, but did not look at it, felt pain and discomfort, but would not acknowledge it. He approached a breaking point, but fortunately, did not disintegrate before his turn to come home.

He had saved his money religiously. With his savings he bought a small house on Pirates Beach. He studiously pursued the acquisition of a dog to be a companion. After research, he purchased a six-week old black Labrador puppy that resembled a warm, fuzzy ball of jet black coal. He named the puppy Maria. Under the warm sun of Pirates Beach he began to relax again. He let the sun bake him while he and the puppy took long walks. He had a job in Detriville that paid well enough and did not demand too much.

Gene Wilson loved his puppy. The two of them romped in the sand and on the beach and in the waves. Gene's daily drive back to the beach after work each day was enjoyable. It gave him time to settle from the work of the day and time to look forward to a walk with Maria, who grew quickly. The summer produced a bond between the two. He often spoke to her, and she listened attentively. Frequently he would glance down at night from his reading and find the dog watching his face. She slept at his bedside, and he acknowledged to himself that it make him feel safer. The nights of the war were fast disappearing and his health was improving. By fall and winter, he was gaining confidence, the job was going well, and he had met a girl at work with whom he talked. If the relationship continued to show promise, he might risk asking her out, but it was too early yet, and he did not yet feel sufficiently secure. In the fall he invested in a small boat. He bought a small, used shotgun.

The purchase of a gun was a brave step for him, but he knew that he had to live and to live meant doing the things that others do. He took one slow cautious step at a time, and the purchase of the shotgun was just such a step. He purposely confined his purchase to a single shot gun. As the weather chilled, he prepared toward hunting in the marshes behind the island. He became adept at paddling the small boat through the marsh grass slipping over the bending tops at high tide. Maria accompanied him, learning to balance in the fragile craft. Occasionally, they would flush a marsh hen. After the shot, she would surge from the boat, which he stabilized against the recoil of her departure. On return he took the hen from her mouth and the two of them performed a literal circus act of getting her back into the boat without tipping. She would shake the water from her coat spraying all surroundings and eliciting a laugh from her master.

Gene Wilson and his dog Maria survived several of these trips that fall, and chuckled about them before the fireside that winter. He was becoming more open, playing the radio more often and selecting good records for the new record player. He took the girl out several times, but carefully avoided any pressure. He could imagine that she was becoming interested, and he began, almost automatically, tidying the house a bit.

The fall and winter were largely gone. Pirates Beach was still gray and lonely in late March, but there was an essence of forthcoming spring. Occasional warm days promoted the memory of previous springs, of warm and hot days, of tanned and laughing children. But until those days appeared, one kept to his sweater or jacket, and made the best of grayness.

Gene Wilson and his dog Maria took a daily walk on the beach. Both looked forward to stretching their muscles, breathing the salt air, feeling the cool and sometimes cold wind of the beach. The man strode the firmer parts of the beach, halfway between high and low water marks, the portion of the beach where the daily pounding of the waves made the sand more compact. The dog, still enjoying the resilient muscles of youth and the irresponsibility of those who can afford to depend on others, romped and ran and jumped and skidded from surf to dunes. She overran the sand crabs, barked at the endless variety of plovers, terns, gulls or pelicans, and generally ran in all directions.

The two left their home on one of these days and turned east. Maria ran toward the surf as if daring the next wave to fall upon the eastern shore of her United States. At the last moment before tearing the wave to fragments, she braked and veered to her left, inclining her body as if she were performing on water skis at Cypress Gardens. Careening like a motorcycle, changing direction, she shifted gears, brought her flywheel back to 4,000 revolutions per minute, gained speed and headed for the dunes to wreak havoc on the pitiless sand crabs.

Running at full tilt as if pursued by dragons and imbued
with the speed of Mercury, she crossed the first dune sending sand
flying as if it were exploding. As she literally flew across the sand, a
circumstance occurred that is possible only for an animal constructed
of the extremely well coordinated substance of which she was born.
As she ran past a small depression in the sand, an unnatural sight and
smell confronted her. Still literally in flight, her head turned to the left
while her body remained in a forward direction. Gene saw it happen.
He was watching her intently, pleased with her health stride and vigor.
He saw her instantaneous diversion and watched as she braked to
an abrupt halt. Now it was the dog who was intent. She had lost the
exhilarated flight of high spirit. Now she was deadly serious, mature
beyond her years. Her instinctive behavior was governed by mental
pathways of which she had no notion. She approached the spot that
had diverted her, walking slowly now, almost cautiously. It was not
so much what she had seen in mid-flight, it was more the smell that
triggered behavior deep in the olfactory lobes of her brain. She had
flown through a chemical cloud, and when she had landed, she was
of a different mood. By this time, Gene had noted her new behavior
and was also approaching the area. He watched as the dog cautiously
stepped forward to within a few feet of the area, then stiffened.
The dog was totally absorbed by a spot in the sand. The sand was
disturbed at this spot, and an object appeared to extend to the surface.
A dozen or so larvae of flies entered and exited through a small hole
in the nearby sand. A stain appeared around the object. A few flies
buzzed. Gene Wilson took in this information visually. He noted the
peculiar behavior of the dog. Obviously someone had buried some

garbage in the sand, or perhaps an animal had died there. He spoke sharply to the dog, he wished her to immediately leave the scene. He turned, but as he did, the aura of the sight, the smell, or both, pierced his memory. Before recall could establish the memory on a screen for inspection, it vanished again into the subconscious.

The man and the dog turned and continued their walk. It was not the same, however, and the return was even more sober. They passed the area walking near the water edge intentionally and continued home for dinner. Later that evening, Gene paused in his reading, and glanced at Maria. He imagined that he discerned a quizzical expression, but dismissed it before allowing it to become a serious thought. Gene's sleep that evening was not as restful as was the usual occasion.

The next day he did not face the walk with the usual enthusiasm, but again did not wish to provide a minor perturbation as a significant event. The dog's behavior left nothing to doubt. She made a direct approach to the spot, again approaching cautiously. Gene called Maria away, and then turned, and calling the dog with him, walked west instead of east. By doing so they would not have to come back along the same route.

For three days they took their walk in a westward direction. It was not unusual to do so, the only difference being that previously they had no particular reason except diversion. On the fourth day, Gene let the dog go eastward, letting her proceed as she wished. While she glanced backward on occasions, she seemed to know that he was allowing her to again inspect the area that troubled both of them. The dog jogged for the block's distance. She then headed into the dunes slowly and deliberately, and she was observing the spot when Gene approached. He looked studiously as if to provide certainty for his previous doubts. He noted that the area was larger and there was definitely a mass in its center. Again, the flies and larvae were present, and this time an odor was unmistakable. He experienced two feelings simultaneously and their synchronization confused him. First, he felt giddy. It seemed that the mass represented something that was vaguely familiar and yet so cloudy that no real image appeared. Secondly, the odor had a sweet, sickening tangibility that was also familiar. He had the sensation that he was repressing the familiarity of both. His action was to turn quickly and call the dog away in an abrupt fashion.

The next day he packed some casual, light clothes, made a call to the plant about a relative's illness, put the dog in the car and drove to the Florida Keys. He and the dog spent five marvelous days in the sun fishing and relaxing. Each time his memory seemed to wish to disturb him, he quickly launched into a new activity until he was relaxed and tired. It was an easy struggle, and the sun and blue water won each time.

At the end of the week he braced himself and turned toward home. He knew that he had a renewed strength and would face whatever seemed to be haunting him. The dog was content.

He spent the weekend rearranging and cleaning the house.

On Monday, April 8, 1974, Gene returned to work. He explained away the tan and healthy appearance amid good natured jokes and teasing. The girl at work was puzzled and cool, and her attitude worried Gene. That afternoon he did not take Maria for a walk, and it was obvious that the dog was confused. Gene felt distinctly guilty, but reassured himself that all would eventually work out properly. The next evening the two went for a walk in a westerly direction.

On Wednesday, Gene let the dog run eastward. Maria ran deliberately down the beach and then at the exact moment, turned into the dunes and came to a halt at the spot. Gene felt weak and sick. He called the dog away and they went home. On Thursday they remained home, with Gene becoming increasingly pensive. Friday's evening news carried a brief description of several young girls having been found in the immediate vicinity bound and gagged. On Saturday, the neighborhood was alive with alarm. Rumors of rape and assault abounded. There were rumors associating Friday's incident with two girls missing since the year before, and one girl missing since February.

On Sunday, Gene Wilson went to church for the first time since childhood. Sitting in the back of the church, wishing to be unnoticed, he vaguely remembered his parents and the rigid necessity of being in church each Sunday morning. He kept his head bowed during most of the service, allowing his soul to plead with the heavens for the strength to face reality. Anyone who would have noticed him leave would have noticed that his face was pale and his eyes were slightly red.

On Monday he went to work, but worked in silence. Others noticed, but his appearance seemed to denote that he wished to be left alone. That afternoon he went home, fed the dog, and sat down to think. Near midnight he crawled into bed.

He called his place of work on Tuesday and reported himself as ill. He carefully attended to his appearance, drank a cup of coffee, got into his car, and drove to the Pirates Beach Police Station.

"I am Eugene Wilson. I live at 808 Adams Street. Every afternoon I go walking with my dog. Recently the dog has been sniffing at some material buried in the dunes in the 900 block. I thought you had better take a look."

The officers looked at Gene quietly. The professionalism in them did not demand an answer or a question. His appearance gave credibility to his statement. Later they would ask the questions.

# Chapter X

R. G. Gooding was chief of police at Pirates Beach. He was a quiet man, serious and attentive. He was neither authoritative nor was he unassuming. He simply came to work each day and did the job well. His men occasionally criticized him but never seriously.

Gooding looked at Gene Wilson as Gene talked and knew that he was troubled.

"Why don't we ride down the beach and look at the place that you are talking about?" He told one of the deputies that he would be right back and walked outside with Gene.

They drove to the 900 block. Gene pointed to the house at 904 Adams. They parked and the chief followed Gene to the front beach. They had used the boardwalk and stopped about twenty feet away from the area to which Wilson pointed. There was a blackened object protruding from the sand that one could easily imagine might represent a human hand. As Wilson turned away the chief noted that he manifested a small shudder. As they rode back to the station Gooding gently asked, "When did you first notice this area?"

"Almost three weeks ago. The dog and I take a walk almost every afternoon. The dog kept sniffing the area. I thought that it might be buried garbage and kept her away from the area. Then I read about the girls and came down to the station."

"When we get to the station, go inside and talk to Deputy Woodbury. He will ask you some questions and have you write a statement. You may leave then. The statement will be typed and you can come back to sign it tomorrow."

Gene went into the station, wrote a statement on a legal pad as instructed, signed it and returned home. He felt weak but distinctly better. He made a decision about brooding upon the matter, called the girl at work, and they decided to go out that evening.

Chief Gooding went into his office and slowly sat at his desk. He asked the secretary to hold any calls. He reached into the right hand desk drawer and withdrew a pad. He realized that his office had just had thrust upon it a major legal responsibility, and he wanted to clearly delineate an overall plan to which he could refer.

He wrote, "9:30 a.m., April 16, 1974. Mr. Eugene Wilson, 808 Adams Street, thirty-four year old male Caucasian, entered the police station and stated that his dog had discovered something buried in the dunes in front of 904 East Adams Street. He requested that we inspect the area. On inspection there appears to be a small human hand protruding from a depressed area in the dunes in front of the boardwalk at 904 East Adams Street. We have not entered the immediate area. Mr. Wilson has filled out a statement."

"10:30 a.m., April 16, 1974. Have discussed situation with Major Flowers. He advises that we turn the entire case over to Detriville Metro. Am attempting to contact Captain Randy Barringer. Have posted Sergeant Brown at the 900 block of Adams until Metro arrives."

"10:40 a.m., April 16, 1974. Contact made with Captain Barringer, who is now on his way here."

When Captain Randolph Barringer received the call at 10:35 a.m. he noted a slight tremor in Gooding's voice. He flipped two switches at the corner of his desk. One of the switches caused a recording of the call on his personal tape recorder. The other caused the call to be recorded on the computer tape downstairs where it was entered with the time and date and could be retrieved in part or whole at any time in the future. He also pulled a pink card from a file on his desk that later would be filled out and entered into his intelligence file. He listened quietly to Gooding. He had always liked Gooding, finding him to be a serious, methodical man. Gooding explained the visit of Eugene Wilson and his ride to the site. He stated that he was not absolutely certain that he was viewing a human hand but it was likely. He mentioned that he had not approached too closely so as to preserve the site as completely as possible. Barringer asked a few questions simply to ascertain Gooding's anticipation. His mind had already focused upon the fact that three young girls had disappeared from Pirates Beach in the past year and that three others had recently been found bound and gagged. Gooding's reply confirmed that both men were considering the missing girls.

Barringer wanted to make a personal inspection before calling forth a full-scale homicide scene mobilization. He informed Gooding that he would be out shortly, agreeing that they would meet at the Pirates Beach Police Station. As he replaced the phone in the cradle, he found Lieutenant Pierce watching him. He nodded, went through his file to find his mobilization list and the two started out of the office together.

"Fielding."

"Yes, sir."

"Get in touch with Bartey and Canthus, tell them to be obtainable. Ivers."

"Yes, sir."

"You and Smith hang tight for a while."

"Yes, sir."

All of them knew something was happening. Any time that the captain and the lieutenant went out together, serious big trouble was brewing somewhere. Moreover, Fielding and Ivers noted the mobilization chart that Barringer was placing into his coat pocket.

Barringer and Pierce drove out to Pirates Beach with Pierce behind the wheel. When he was asked to drive, Pierce knew that the captain wanted to think or observe, and he remained silent until he was addressed. As they drove across the causeway, Barringer was first intent upon the marsh, then on the sky, and then began his perpetual habit of writing notes to himself. When the two of them were together, Barringer shared his notes verbally with Pierce. Pierce always considered this sharing as a teaching exercise although there occurred many times when he did not understand the nature of the notations. At such times he did not intrude with questions, fearful of breaking the apparent depth of concentration of which Barringer was capable.

"High tide."

"Yes, sir."

"Check tides and weather of any day in question."

"Yes, sir."

"Not only check tides but cross-check wind effect on the tides on that day."

"Yes, sir."

"One causeway onto the island."

"Yes, sir."

"Poor choice of disposal site to anyone either not living on the island or not intimately familiar with it."

"Yes sir, except crime of passion occurring on the island itself."

"Good, Pierce."

Pierce felt good at the compliment, for it was rare for him to comment upon the captain's discussions. But this time he had risked it and come out on top. He accelerated the car.

"Not so fast."

"Yes, sir."

Barringer had his window down. It was a spring day, and the air across the salt march felt invigorating. A black skimmer could be seen fishing one of the many tidal creeks. Its lower beak barely touched the water as it flew effortlessly down the creek. Occasionally it would rise and soar over a small amount of marsh and then re-enter the creek as if it were a torpedo plane searching on a dangerous mission. Far overhead a pair of terns practiced aerial acrobatics flying wing tip to wing tip, swerving and soaring as if practicing to join the Blue Angels.

"Need to determine the population, income brackets, seasonal census, crime records of the island. Reserve an airplane for an overflight, or better, call Jim Rogers for his helicopter."

They were over the causeway now and onto Main Street. Within two blocks they stopped, and the two men went inside the concrete block building that served as the Pirates Beach Police Station.

"Hello, Dick, good to see you again."

"Thanks, Randy, you are looking well. How is Jenny?"

"Great, thanks. What have we got?"

"Well, as I said over the phone, this guy Wilson walks in here this morning and tells us about three weeks ago his dog notices something in the dunes while they were out on their usual walk. Wilson doesn't think much about it except that it happens again. Then Wilson reads about our episode last week with the three girls and begins to slowly put things together. He comes in here today and tells us that we better take a look."

"He make a statement?"

"Yeah, it's right here, hasn't been typed yet."

Barringer looked at the yellow legal note pad. The pages were not rumpled and still attached to the pad, clean, unstained. The writing was fairly bold, neat, orderly. The lettering was smooth and full. The letters tended to be slanted to the right. The crosses of the ts were flat. The periods were above the lines of the yellow pad. He began to read. The sentences were relatively short. Wilson tended to be explicit. There were few adjectives. The vocabulary was varied and there was remarkably little repetition of the same words. His experiences were succinctly stated but adequately described the case, the account being successive but not chronological in the sense of relating to exact times or dates.

Gooding watched Barringer read. He had always heard of Barringer's unusual intellect but he considered it rather peculiar for a man reputed to be so smart to read so slowly. He had even noted that at first Barringer didn't seem to be reading but rather just looking at the pad. Peculiar fellow, Barringer.

When Randy had finished the statement he asked Gooding for a copy. Gooding again replied that he would have it typed. Barringer said that he preferred a copy as it was, and Gooding had one made. He considered Barringer a bit impatient.

Gooding got into the rear of Barringer's car, Pierce still driving. They drove to 903 Adams. Sergeant Brown met them there.

"Sergeant Brown, you know Lieutenant Pierce and Captain Barringer."

"Yes, sir. Good to see you both again. Nothing happening, chief."

Barringer shook hands with Brown. "Good to see you again, Sergeant. Would you do me a favor and park your cruiser over there? I would like to have someone watching the area but from a distance so as not to cause too much curiosity." He motioned to an empty driveway half a block away. At that location it would appear that Sergeant Brown was simply performing a traffic surveillance.

"Be glad to, Captain."

Barringer opened the trunk of his car. He removed a small step-ladder that he had placed there before they left the station. He then removed a pair of binoculars and a compact 35mm camera. He deftly applied a 40mm lens leaving the usual 50mm lens in the car. He rechecked the presence of a new roll of black and white film. Finally he dropped a 200mm lens in his jacket pocket and turned to Gooding. "Dick, I know that I have peculiar ways, but if you will be patient with me, I'll promise that it will work out."

Gooding knew Barringer's reputation for thoroughness.

"Sure. No sweat."

"I want you to show me from here exactly where you and Wilson walked this morning."

They were standing at the rear of Barringer's car. Gooding pointed out the area at the end of the boardwalk and the path that he and Wilson had used to approach it. Barringer snapped a couple of shots with the wide angle lens. He then told Pierce to stay at the car with Gooding, which was his way of telling Gooding that he wished to approach the scene alone. The two watched as Barringer began his approach carrying the binoculars, the camera, and the ladder. They watched him stop a dozen times, taking photographs, occasionally mounting the ladder, peering into the surrounding area, apparently interested in everything but the scene in question. Finally on the boardwalk about twenty feet away, he stopped, looking at his feet. Gooding noted that he was almost exactly at the point at which he and Wilson had stopped, but it was inconceivable that he had left foot prints on a thin layer of sand blown upon the boardwalk. They watched as Barringer again unfolded his ladder and sat upon it. They watched as he once again surveyed the entire scene and photographed in all directions. He then looked intently at the area of the dunes. He lifted his binoculars and examined the dunes at length. As Gooding's impatience mounted, they saw Barringer finally change his lens on the camera and photograph the entire area. When finished he again raised the glasses, and with painstaking minuteness, searched all of the closely surrounding area.

They had been at the scene for nearly an hour. It appeared to Gooding that much of it was devoid of any reasonable activity. Pierce knew better, but simply watched and chatted amicably with Gooding on any subject other than the captain. They had turned away from the scene, and suddenly, Barringer appeared at their elbows. His quiet approach startled Gooding and amused Pierce.

"What did you see?"

"Nothing much. It is a young girl. She has been there a couple of months. Could be Mary Brady. The cold has done much to preserve the body. She was buried hastily. It is a daytime burial, so we are dealing with a very irrational, highly disturbed person. There is a good bit more, but I would like to initiate a full-scene investigation. We had better get on with it."

Pierce took pleasure in Gooding's face. He knew that Gooding was trying to mentally determine if Barringer was faking, trying to flabbergast him, or was actually as positive as he appeared to be. Pierce had watched others in the same predicament. As for himself, he knew what was happening and awaited the flow of orders and instructions.

As they drove back to the station, instructions began, slow and methodical with emphasis placed so that they would be remembered.

The instructions were not orders and were not requests. They were a series of steps of approach to a problem, and Pierce knew too well that they had better be done correctly.

"First, let Chief Gooding off at the station. Secondly, stop at that little place that we passed on the other side of the causeway for a quick sandwich. We'll call Jim Rogers for the helicopter. He can pick me up from the field in back of the station. While I'm on the overflight, start the scene plan. Rope off where we parked the car, straight to the beach below the high-water mark. Then go eastward with the rope to beyond the next house and back out to the road and back to the starting point. Get in touch with Lanny Brooks. Tell him you're calling for me and that we might need him and his bulldozer this afternoon. Call Joe McCarthy. Nobody else unless he is away. If he is, ask Jean Jacobs."

"Yes, sir."

"Chief, could we leave Sergeant Brown there a little longer? I'll have one of my crew out within an hour."

"Sure."

They dropped Chief Gooding at the station. Gooding went back to his note pad and began again. He called the mayor again and informed him that he had turned the entire investigation over to Metro. He told the mayor that Barringer thought it was a young girl, but that he considered Barringer to be a bit slow and somewhat speculative.

Pierce called the dispatcher and had her call Jim Rogers. Jim would have the small Bell helicopter in the field behind the station by the time of their arrival. Pierce radioed to Fielding at the station.

"800 to 806."

"806."

"Send 807 to 227 Apple. Ask 807 to I.V. Blue Knight."

Pierce had used the division's special code designed by Barringer. 806 was Fielding, 807 was Ivers. 227 Apple was a point in a finely constructed coordinate system for Detriville County. One could determine a specific house or location anywhere in the county using the coordinate system. Further, each police automobile in the division was equipped with a mini-computer that operated on two radio beams at right angles to each other, and which would establish a visual display of the exact location of the car at any time. During surveillance or pursuit, an officer only had to glance at his dashboard to radio his location to others.

Pierce had instructed Fielding to send Ivers to 803 Adams and to interview Sergeant Brown at that location. Pierce then reached down and changed his radio channel. At its new setting, his car radio triggered an electronic circuit at the station that operated a recording system for the division. It was a system designed for any type of note-taking activity.

"This is 800 crossing point 219 Andy. Notation for weather and moon check on day of interest. Cross check both. Check census 200A and related demographic data. Check softball. Operate Mobile Six with special attention to Medicare."

He, using rather cryptographic references, reminded himself of his duties as previously instructed by Barringer. If he should have an accident or not be available, his division could decipher most if not all of his intentions. In this way, information was seldom lost, and retrieval was possible to recheck data that could have been possibly passed over before or was lost to the fickle human memory.

As Pierce and Barringer drove into the field behind the station, they saw ahead of them a man standing beside a flying machine.

The man was small and wiry and was dressed in dark green pants and a tan shirt giving him a semi-official appearance. He was darkly tanned, wore dark glasses, and seemed to be absorbed in his machine. The chopper was a small bubble type helicopter, appearing to be perched beside the man as if it were a friendly, giant dragonfly. Its wings were gently rotating and its motor gave a soft rumble. Barringer strode towards the machine with his binoculars and camera slung over his shoulder. Pierce left towards the station. Barringer had to duck beneath the rotors under which Rogers walked with ease. They nodded to each other, climbed into opposite sides of the bubble, and both adjusted belts, earphones, and microphones. Barringer checked his camera as Rogers lifted his machine towards Pirates Beach.

A seagull slipped by in a downstream current, amazed at the loud giant bird that had swallowed one man only a half an hour ago, and now contained two of the humans, the second even larger than the first.

Pierce entered the station to find Fielding, Smith, Bartey, and Canthus waiting, aware of some action in the wind.

"Okay, find your Mobile Sixes."

The men went to their separate sources of documents and found the manual referred to and began their individual inspection of its contents. Pierce had gone to his desk and found his copy.

"A body has been found at Pirates Beach by a man walking his dog. The dog kept sniffing at one spot, and finally the man became suspicious. After he heard of the three girls last week he put two and two together and came in today. The captain inspected the area. We are going to rope off a large area and go to Mobile Six. The captain wants Joe McCarthy. If McCarthy is not available, get Dr. Jacobs. The captain wants Lanny Brooks standing by with his bulldozer. Get Davis to dig up the body. Now let's go through Mobile Six."

Fielding had written down Pierce's instruction. The men now turned to their manuals, which described Mobile Six.

Mobile Six was a mobilization plan. It depicted the steps to be taken at a murder scene. It began with the initial inspection to ascertain the presence of a body. It then described the isolation techniques of cordoning off the appropriate area and the stationing of personnel to insure isolation. These personnel were men who intently watched the crime scene investigator as he worked the scene. They made notes of his direction of approach to the body, the photographic sequence, the removal of evidence, and the establishment of measured points of reference from the body to the objects found in relation to the body. They established a grid describing the entire area, including trees, shrubbery, and lines of visual sight. They each photographed the investigation as it proceeded. The manual described the sequence of calling the coroner, the medical examiner, and a crime scene investigator, notifying the chief and the operations major, and dealing with the press and the solicitor.

The men rehearsed their plans for an hour, each detailing Pierce's instructions as to their individual roles. The probable time at the scene was calculated, the night shift security of the area was determined, and the method of restraint of the press was given attention. Then the afternoon's activities were calculated as best possible.

When Pierce was thoroughly satisfied with plans for deployment, he set a starting time. The rest would go like clockwork. Finally, he established a conference time at the station that night for review of the day's activities. He could hear the chopper approaching the field and hastened to meet Barringer.

"Get it all done?"

"Yes, sir."

"How did it go?"

"Piece of cake."

# Chapter XI

"Did you get Dr. McCarthy?"

"Yes, sir, told him to meet us at the scene at two o'clock."

"How about Lanny Brooks?"

"Yes, sir, standing by with his bulldozer."

"Dr. Davis ready?"

"I'll pick up Dr. Davis at the museum."

"Who is photographing?"

"McCullum."

"Good, damn good. Did you see that duck scene of his?"

"Yes, sir, he's gonna put it in that big contest up in Maryland."

"I'll bet on him."

"Me, too."

"That clock's not right, is it?"

"No, sir."

"See that they correct that clock, four minutes could make or break."

"Yes, sir."

"I've got to stop by and brief the chief. Meet you at the scene at two. Nobody moves until McCullum is through with preliminaries."

"Yes, sir."

"Barbara, is the chief in?"

"Yes, Captain, but he's on the way out to lunch and in an awful mood."

"I'll have to chance it. I need to brief him on something."

"Could it wait till after lunch?"

"'Fraid not."

"Chief, Captain Barringer is here, says he needs to brief you on something. I told him. He says its necessary. I'll call and tell them you've been delayed and will meet them at one-thirty. Go on in, Captain, but look out."

"Good morning, Chief."

"Good morning, Randy, sit down. What's up?"

"Chief, at about 9:00 a.m., a man named Eugene Wilson walked into the Pirates Beach Police Station and made a statement concerning a suspicious circumstance on the beach. Wilson walks his dog on the beach every day. He had noticed that the dog was sniffing at one spot in the dunes in the 900 block of Adams Street repeatedly. This morning we investigated and found what appears to be a human hand protruding from the sand. I investigated at the request of Chief Gooding. It does appear to be a hand, possibly that of a young girl. If you will remember, there have been reports of three missing girls from Pirates Beach in the past year. Last year, two teenage girls named Clair and Lawton disappeared one evening. Two months ago, a child named Mary Brady disappeared, and last week three girls were found tied beneath a house not far from this scene."

"You suspect that this is the Brady child?"

"Yes, sir."

"What's your next step?"

"I'm going to Mobile Six, and plan to be at the scene at two o'clock."

"Okay, Randy, I've got to have lunch with the administrator. Has the press caught on yet?"

"Not that I know of. I've used code so far, but I'll have to break that soon."

"I'll be downtown, probably at the cafeteria. I'll get out about two-thirty, quarter-to-three. Did Gooding sign off to us?"

"Yes, sir."

"The 900 block?"

"Yes, sir."

"See you there. Be careful Randy, the other graves could be nearby."

"Yes sir, I've roped off a big area."

"Good."

Barringer walked slowly back to the office, his head down, lost in thought. The hallway was cold, impersonal. There was a water fountain, a clock, and a series of closed doors to offices. Occasionally the hall would occupy an officer herding someone who had thrown dice with the legal rules of human behavior and lost. Most of the losers looked the same, tousled, humorless, furtive. Most were silent in this hallway as they were led to one of the offices to make a statement of their wrongs. Most were busy trying to remember sufficient details of a lie to make it seem like some semblance of the truth. Those that were not thinking beyond the realm of truth were probably not thinking much at all, a condition which is probably as good as any to explain their presence in this stolid hallway of losers.

Barringer glanced at the clock and made a four minute mental correction. It was 12:50 p.m. He entered a door at the end of the hall, which opened into an office complex. In the open area were multiple desks generally occupied by his investigative team and the secretarial help. Barringer had a fairly spacious office to one side, which was adjoined by a conference room. Toward the back was a smaller room for coffee and a refrigerator. A coat room, a bathroom, and a supply area completed the office complex. Near the offices were the files and a small computer that provided an excellent intelligence unit.

Barringer's office was austere except for the books. The desk was an old oak desk that he had salvaged and refinished. A nearby table was largely covered with neatly arranged stacks of papers or folders. His desk was subtly arranged to have light or to use light in attending the person who sat in front of it. Two straight but comfortable chairs were in front of the desk, and a third could be used but was rarely necessary. The person who sat in front of this desk seldom knew the extent to which they were watched and did not know that they were occasionally photographed and almost always recorded. The telephone had numerous attachments and an extensive keyboard. It was a communication marvel. On the back of the desk was a series of silent mercury switches that controlled a camera, several sets of buzzers to other desks, two tape recorders, and a portion of the office computer.

Barringer sat at the desk and dialed the office of Dr. Joseph McCarthy at the Detriville University of Medicine.

"Joan, this is Randy Barringer. Is he there?"

"Yes, sir, how have you been?"

"Great, the spring brings me alive. How about you?"

"Fine. Just a minute, I'll get him."

"Hi, Randy, what you got?"

"It looks like it could be one of the missing girls on Pirates Beach, probably Mary Brady."

"How do you want to work it?"

"That's what I'm calling about. I thought we ought to let Dr. Davis in on it. What do you think?"

"Sure, Randy. It's early enough. God, is he slow."

"But good."

"Yeah, I agree. What do you want me to do?"

"Well, I really would appreciate it if you could be there at the beginning. I know it's slow, but if you could, it's always better."

"Who'll go first, photography?"

"Yeah, I've got McCullum."

"Excellent, you seen his birds?"

"Yeah, they're great."

"The Brady girl's been missing several months?"

"Yeah, missing since February twenty-first."

"How about the other girls?"

"Almost exactly a year."

"Near the same location?"

"Yep."

"What do you think about other graves?"

"That's why I want you and Dr. Davis."

"Okay. What time?"

"Two o'clock okay?"

"Sure."

"Pierce will pick you up. I'll see you there."

"Okay, see you."

Barringer sat quietly. It was one o'clock. At one-fifteen he fixed himself a cup of coffee and returned to his desk. Dr. Davis would excavate the child and turn her over to Dr. McCarthy. McCarthy would do a preliminary exam. He would then place the partially decomposed body into a special set of supporting cushions to keep the body as it had been when uncovered. When the university van with the body left, he would prepare himself to ask Dr. Davis to establish a grid of excavation of the remainder of the roped off area. The Chief of Detriville police would be present as would the county administrator, both to be certain that they were well-enough informed to speak correctly to the press.

The press. Barringer sighed. Maybe they would send Susan. The television crews would appear by magic. Dave Goodman would smile and ask questions. He would try his best to create emotion and conflict. Hank Ansley would try to ask intelligent questions, but would never quite make it. Well, that's life.

Barringer considered the possible approach of darkness. It all had to be today. He set six o'clock as a deadline for Lanny Brooks and the bulldozer.

He mentally prepared for a summary session that evening. The other agencies would have to be notified, but he would leave that to the chief.

Most of what he considered was already written down, but he made himself rehearse it anyhow. Finally, he wrote the major aspects of his thoughts into his small notebook, stuck it back in his pocket, and prepared to go to the beach. As he turned from his office, his eyes strayed across the violent crimes part of his book shelf. Infrared photography caught his attention, but his attention was arrested on the book by Shabel entitled *Pattern Recognition*. He had placed this book in the violent crime section to remind himself of the necessity of watching for patterns of behavior among violent criminals. Surely the perpetrator of the murders now apparently unfolding was a creature of pattern, probably helpless to the pattern of his own life, maybe helpless to a pattern that had been established long before he was born.

Barringer drove toward the beach, noting the tide. Out in the marsh an egret stood, balanced on one leg. The egret appeared to have shoulders slumped like an old man's shoulders, tired and apathetic. The head and back were slumped into the shoulders, and for all the world the egret appeared to be an old man in a baseball cap simply standing on one foot watching the cars go by.

Barringer smiled and then became serious again.

Dr. Daniel Davis was an archeologist. He had worked with Jamison on the Mesopotamian ruins and had earned international fame for his methods of preservation of sandstone artifacts. He had retired in Detriville because of the museum. The city had given him the keys to the museum, and for all practical purposes, he owned it. He was present at most intellectual gatherings in Detriville and received distinguished visitors from all over the world. He was in his late sixties, was small, wiry, and neat as a pin, and had snow white hair and tanned, healthy features. His blue eyes sparkled and saw what they looked at. His attention span was endless, and his perception as keen as a razor.

"Hello, Randy."

"Hello, Dr. Davis. Appreciate your coming out."

"Glad to. Is it one of the missing girls?"

"Yes sir, I'm afraid so. At least that's what I think at the moment."

"How would you like me to function?"

"I've roped off this entire area with the consideration that the other two missing girls could be nearby. I would like to let McCullum begin his photography right away, and then have you begin with the body. When we excavate, I'd like to turn the body over to McCarthy and begin a search of the grave site. After that, if you agree, I'd like your advice about constructing a grid of the entire site. I'm pressed by circumstances to look for the other bodies, even to the extent of bringing in large equipment."

Dr. Davis made a face, and Barringer laughed.

"Sorry to say a bad word like that, but I'm in a bind."

"I'm just kidding, Randy. But you have to make me a promise that you'll never let them get a bulldozer within a mile of my grave."

"It's a solemn promise. I'll protect your body with my life."

"Randy, may I talk to McCullum and suggest a few shots?"

"Absolutely, you're in charge."

Randy Barringer smiled as the older, smaller man walked away to talk to the photographer. He watched the little man and his old equipment satchel, remembering how lucky he had been to interest the famous curator in this grisly type of work. He had gone to the museum years ago, shortly after Dr. Davis had arrived in Detriville. He had been confronted with an old case involving a gangland murder.

Evidence had been abundant that the victim had been severely beaten and probably murdered but his body had never been found. After years, friction in the gang led to information about the probable grave site. Barringer had known that the case rested on a meticulous uncovering of the victim and preservation of all evidence. He had decided on asking Dr. Davis to perform a forensic archeological task. Dr. Davis had politely listened to him and then asked to be allowed to think it over. The next day Randy had called. Dr. Davis gently explained his terms, which consisted in the main of a rigid demand for patience. Randy had wisely conceded. Shortly thereafter Dr. Davis became an official member of the team. Everyone was made properly aware that if Dr. Davis was brought into a case, everything else waited. And wait they did, in the rain, in the cold, at night by lantern swatting mosquitoes or standing around drinking cold coffee. They always waited on the most meticulous, most methodological man they had ever seen. Davis was an expert.

McCullum listened to Dr. Davis. He loved the old man. No one else appreciated light and angles the way Davis did. He made beautiful use of shadows, and special photography such as infrared and complex filters. He wanted truth, and he always wanted detail. McCullum listened carefully.

When Davis was finished, McCullum went to work.

Henry McCullum was a highly successful photographer. His father had given him a Brownie camera when he was twelve years old. The boy and the Brownie lived together. Without film they took thousands of photographs. With an occasional roll of film they produced photographs that won all local contests. By fourteen, he had been given an excellent camera by the local newspaper as an award for several exceptional photographs that he had given the paper. At sixteen, he won national contests. During the summer between high school years, he worked at a local photography shop and learned the arts of development and printing. After studying art in college, he joined the Air Force and learned the photographic technologies associated with high-speed spectral analysis at long distance and other strategic problems. The service involved him in investigating low-light-level lenses and high-resolution infrared photography. After four years in the service, he returned to Detriville to begin a successful career in professional photography. He loved his art to entertain, to teach, to beautify, enthrall, provide confidence, preserve, document, and to satisfy himself.

Years previously a young police lieutenant named Barringer had asked for an appointment. He had been faced with a rather large, apparently intelligent serious police officer with a huge scar on the right side of his face. He had initial difficulty paying attention to the lieutenant's explanation because of his focus of attention on the scar and the effect that it had on the facial features. He was fascinated with the idea to provide a remarkable portrait. Finally, he was made to listen. The lieutenant explained three challenging law enforcement problems. One concerned the sale of drugs at night to teenagers, the next was a surveillance problem, and the third was documentation of a violent crime scene under poor light and at close quarters. As he listened to Barringer, he became caught in the absorbing complexities of photography under adverse circumstances. Each problem that Barringer explained had about it a circumstance of impossibility, and yet there was always a slight possibility that it could be done by an expert. He had thought of that conversation many times. Eventually, years later, he came to understand that Barringer had trapped him, but by that time so many extraordinary events had been experienced, so many satisfactions of an impossible job well-accomplished, so many fights against the enemy won that the he was glad he had lost the first battle and was eventually helping win the war. He was a member of the team, and the cops loved him. He had always taken time to snap the human side of their work and to include them to give credit in an undeniable fashion. They would do anything for him and eagerly waited to see how each photograph turned out. They held his equipment, they strung his lines for his lights, they went back to the shop for more film, they chauffeured him, and they treated him like the artist he was.

After talking to Davis, McCullum began his part of the job at the grave scene. First, he photographed where they were. He included the surrounding people, the houses, street signs, the beach, and the ocean. He was careful to include the inevitable onlookers. Twice before, his photographs had shown the criminal standing in the crowd, having come back to watch the police work at his crime. Very little escaped McCullum's camera. He next began to take general views of the scene, careful to show the boardwalk across the dunes, the nearby vacant house, the door to the shower slightly ajar. Next he began on Dr. Davis's requests, and strange they were. Davis had explained that three to four months previously, the prevailing winds would have been northerly ones, blowing sand from the general direction to which he pointed. Davis next withdrew a beautiful small pocket compass from his old satchel and showed McCullum certain angles related to the compass from which he requested photographs be made. His other request related to the light produced by the time of day. He divided the day into early morning, mid-noon, late afternoon, and early darkness. He requested McCullum to shoot the scene from vantage points related to the way that light from these times would have allowed the assailant to see the spot where some child was to be buried. McCullum liked Davis. Davis understood light and views and angles. He liked that.

McCullum was finished at about 3:00 p.m. He finished by surreptitiously photographing the onlookers again. He nodded to Davis who had been patiently watching his every move. Dr. Daniel Davis nodded back. He respected McCullum. He had rarely seen equal photographic skill. McCullum's documentary of the museum and the close ups of the cambrian fossils were very satisfying. Davis walked to the spot where an apparent human hand was protruding from the sand. He carried his small, low folding canvas stool and the old satchel. Two officers brought a weathered trunk from the back of Pierce's car. Davis carefully approached the site and put down the stool and the satchel several feet away from the site. He opened the satchel, withdrew a leather-bound note pad, and began writing. He motioned to the officers that the trunk be placed near him, and they retreated. He next opened the trunk, withdrew a numbered file, and placed some of the nearby sand in it. He scribbled in the pad. He then began meticulously removing sand from the body.

The chief had arrived and the administrator with him. The press had arrived and they tackled the chief and the administrator.

They knew better than to approach Barringer except through the chief. The chief knew well to be cautious at this time, and he kept referring all questions possible to the administrator. Both of the older men enjoyed the challenge of the press, and the press simply had to be patient.

Barringer was everywhere. His eyes occasionally searched for Dr. McCarthy, who was inexplicably late. Barringer inspected the onlookers carefully. He wrote constantly in his plastic covered legal pad. He noted and described each house in the nearby area, directed a half dozen men to document every tree, each fence, and each path, and to measure the alignment of all parts to each other with a steel tape, thereby constructing a map.

Pierce had directed a telephone lineman to provide a temporary phone stall and had the power company installing temporary power circuits to support powerful lighting for the evening if necessary.

Barringer walked the beach, occasionally stopping to jot something onto the legal pad. He would occasionally stop, retrace his steps in a measured fashion, then turn and walk through his paces again. He approached the scene from every possible direction, each time stopping to intently observe Dr. Davis's progress.

Dr. McCarthy arrived. He hurriedly found Barringer.

"Sorry, Randy. I got caught."

"Figured so, Joe—not like you to let us get too far ahead."

Both men laughed, but Dr. McCarthy was already intently searching the scene for the form of Dr. Davis. He spotted him and watched for a moment.

"Anything more definite, Randy?"

"Yes, as I told you over the phone, it seems to be the body of Mary Brady who disappeared about four months ago. She appears to have been clad in panties and tied with what appears to be clothesline. Davis should be through in about an hour. Joe, I would really appreciate anything you could tell us tonight. The number of girls involved indicate a local situation, and I would really like to stay ahead of the news people."

"Sure, I understand. Anything special?"

"Yes, the rope is terribly important. As many photographs as possible before you remove it. Close ups of the knots, the rope ends, the sequence of tying, and any relationship of the rope to death. We should look for any signs of torture, previous rope burns, gag material, that type of thing."

"Okay."

"Joe, one other thing. I've got a sneaking suspicion from what I've seen so far that she wasn't violently molested. The presence of the panties attest to that, but there is a hole in the panties. Please look carefully for any foreign material in the vagina and the rectum. I'm afraid we're dealing with a real sicko here, and that makes it more important that we put the hustle on."

"Okay, Randy."

"Well, I'm holding you up. I've left work with Pierce to apply the body packs when Davis is through and transport exactly as exhumed, but I'll leave all that to you."

"Okay, Randy. I'll go hustle the distinguished old curator."

"Not too much, Joe. He gives us an awful lot."

"I know."

Dr. Joseph McCarthy walked back to his car, opened the trunk and took out a large weathered camera bag and a folding stool. Dr. McCarthy was the medical examiner for Detriville County. Twenty years previously, he had been one of the university's best medical students. He established a near-record achievement by essentially working twenty-four hours a day for four straight years as a student, and five more as a pathology resident and fellow. McCarthy had two unique traits that accounted for his professional and personal successes. He focused on one thing at a time, completing each task to perfection, and manifested a patience and persistence beyond belief. When he turned to one of his scouts to explain a problem, that problem got explained so thoroughly that it never required being redone. When he was through with one person, another would be waiting, and so it went, on and on, until everything was complete or all were so tired that they left him to his eventual rest. The next day was the same, and the day after that. In his professional life, he exhibited such remarkable thoroughness, such attention to detail, that each case yielded maximum information. He became widely known as an unusually competent forensic pathologist and was consulted throughout the state. His colleagues wrote his papers, and together they shared academic fame.

Tonight he would carefully aid in the packing and transportation of the figure that Davis had almost finished uncovering. He would meet the transport vehicle at the university hospital and supervise the transportation up to the autopsy room and the unpacking. There, with his resident staff and with the police officer in residence, he would carefully study the unearthed figure. Placed on a high, central, stainless steel table in a large tiled and silent room beneath a myriad of incandescent lighting, the figure would be in a position exactly similar to that assumed when it was uncovered. McCarthy would silently study the figure from all possible angles, occasionally photographing, occasionally sketching, occasionally dictating into a central dictating machine. He would be occasionally examining with a large lens, occasionally readjusting a light, but always wondering, questioning, examining all possibilities. His staff would have left during this time knowing the extraordinary lengths of time consumed, learning little in this process, and often wondering whether some of this was a waste of time. Later they would return and assist in the dissection and the examination of tissues, again geared to McCarthy's apparent complete disdain for time. When they added almost everything, they wondered why he was so great. When they added in the score, the greatness was apparent.

McCarthy swung the camera bag over his shoulder and carried it and the folding stool to a spot sufficiently near the shallow grave site where a famous museum curator had nearly completed blowing, whisking, and gently brushing small amounts of the sand of Pirates Beach from the figure of a young girl.

"Good evening, Dr. Davis."

"Good evening, Joe."

"Anything nearby?"

"Not that I've found. Looks like the grave was dug in a hurried fashion using a flat shovel, possibly the type used for shoveling coal. See those marks? They are too sharp to be attributed to anything but a well-constructed shovel. I haven't seen any accompanying material except for those clothes."

"Anything I should watch for?"

"Not that isn't more apparent to you than to me. After all, I'm just an old grave digger. You're the doctor."

"Had I been a real doctor, all my patients would occupy your diggings. How's it look for my scout troop at the museum?"

"Looks good. The shipment will be in on the first. It'll take me two weeks to unpack it and form the exhibit. You and I will let the troop in right after church on the second weekend, and we'll have them for two hours before we open to the general public that afternoon."

"Great! We're all looking forward to it."

Davis stopped his work to rest for a minute and slowly edged himself onto the edge of the crater he had been excavating. He looked for a few minutes at the small contorted figure in front of him and then he looked at the beach and finally out onto the quiet ocean.

"Joe, we'll never learn to prevent violence, but we should learn to prevent its reoccurrence."

"Yes sir, we should."

# Chapter XII

"Pierce."

"Sir."

"Put the word out. Conference at eight o'clock."

"Yes sir. Who do you want?"

"All of our people. Dr. Davis. I'll speak to him before he leaves. Dr. McCarthy. I'll call him. Chief Gooding and any of his force who might know the island people well. You go invite the mayor of Pirates Beach. I want him to know we'll be all over his place. Contact Mrs. Barr at the library. I want her to research possible related events for us. I'll talk to her."

"How about the other chiefs?"

"I'll let our chief invite them."

"Any street people?"

"No, not yet. I want to try and get this case organized in reference to the past two year's investigation."

"Yes, sir."

"Pierce."

"Yes, sir."

"I'm going to stop at Chief Gooding's office and interview Patrolman Owens. He's the one who found the three girls bound and gagged two weeks ago. I'll go from there to the autopsy room and see if McCarthy has anything for us. I'll stop for a sandwich at the hospital, run by the library and talk to Margaret Barr, and then go to the conference room and set up. I hear there's a rape in the sunset area and two break-ins on the Hill. Get Simmons and Smith to cover those and use over-time if necessary. I want complete freedom for this one, for about twenty-four hours. Okay."

"Yes, sir. Captain?"

"Yes, Pierce."

"How about Dr. Stevenson?"

"No, Pierce. I thought about it, but this one is too flakey as yet. If we solve it, I might ask him to put the pieces together."

"Captain, why do you use him sometimes, and not others?"

"It's a feeling, Pierce. He's good when there is a need for critical examination of what is true and what isn't, for logic and reasoning, for the true who-dun-it. I've got a feeling that this one is a hunt for some sort of twisted animal, somebody who preys on fearful, small people. I think Dr. Rider is going to be more appropriate here."

"Yes, sir."

"Pierce."

"Yes, sir."

"Thanks for taking charge today. It allows me the ability to remain free to follow small leads. It's good for me to have you to depend on."

"Yes, sir."

Pierce's shoulders moved an inch higher, his head was straighter. He turned from the captain and began looking for his men. *Can you imagine that, the captain saying he was dependent on him.* He began rephrasing the comment in preparation for telling his wife. When he eventually got off work, his wife would join him in the kitchen and fix coffee and cake or pie, and ask him about his day or days and nights. He would unload, and she would attend carefully. She was magic at this part of their marriage, and it kept him healthy and prideful. He reflected for a moment and then began organizing his part of the job to come.

Barringer drove to the Pirates Beach police headquarters. He sought out Patrolman Owens and listened attentively to his account of finding three young girls bound and gagged beneath stairs to a beach house two weeks previously in the vicinity of Mary Brady's grave. He then obtained the statement of the event written by Owens at the time of the occurrence. He mentally calculated the consistency of the two accounts and found no significant discrepancy.

"You say that you got a call about a surfing infraction?"

"Yes, sir."

Barringer knew there would be no other record of that call. In his own area, the call would have been taped, timed, and dated. Ordinarily he would check the call to corroborate, even if it had been his own patrolman.

"Who was the caller?"

"Mrs. Hamilton lives two houses away, and she was right. There were two boys surfing in front of her house, which is a quarter mile away from the surfing permitted area. I had parked at the best access area when I spotted the girls. No one else was in sight. Of course, I forgot the surfers when I saw the girls."

"Did anyone ever talk to the surfers later?"

"Yes, sir."

"And?"

"One of them had noticed the girls. He had even thought about trying to meet them, but the water was cold and he figured his buddy would think he was trying to pansy out."

"Did he see anyone else?"

"No, sir."

"Surfers only see what they want to, huh?"

"Yes, sir."

He gently questioned Owens for the next twenty minutes on every observation that Owens had made. He asked about the girls' fear, the reliability of their description, about the round scar on the assailant's leg, the type of rope used to bind the girls, the method of gagging them and questions that Owens could not conceive of as relevant to the event. When they had finished, Owens could feel a light perspiration.

No one had asked him half the questions he had just answered. He would remember for many years the possibility of having to answer to the details of his observations and for many years his observations would be more detailed. When they finished he understood Barringer's reputation. He had learned, and he had the feeling that the captain had intentionally taught him. When Barringer finally stood up, thanked him, and shook his hand, Owens thanked Barringer, genuinely.

Barringer left for the autopsy room. He admittedly disliked going to the autopsy room. He felt confined in the hospital except for the emergency room. The autopsy room represented the end point in the hospital. It was a drab, sterile, lifeless room, despite the pathologists. There was always a pervading sense of the ultimate doom, the end of life. The instruments were grim. The students who watched were always pale, some of them nervous, others appearing half sick. The bodies, which in life had produced music, athletics, laughter, jokes, and tears, lay as completely naked as can be displayed. Moreover, they were open, and so they were naked outside and inside. Barringer often wondered what the doctors thought in the autopsy room. They didn't seem to think much at all. They just seemed programmed to do their gruesome tasks of splitting other people open and peering inside. Barringer often wondered what doctors thought about most of the time. Nurses, he guessed, at least outside the autopsy room.

He turned his attention to the marsh as he crossed the causeway. Vietnam always rattled back into consciousness when he crossed the marsh. The tidal marshes were identical to the rice fields in Vietnam. There had been a saying there, "Live like the grass. Bend with the wind. Bend and you will not break." The tidal creeks reminded him of the miles of rice ditches that he had hidden and traveled in, often barefoot, in short pants, protecting his weapons of lethality. Each summer he provided himself with ample return to the warm ooze of the tidal creeks. The bad portions of old memories had long disappeared in the pleasant return to nature, the abundant harvest of fish, shrimp, oysters, and clams. He loved the out-of-doors, and the salty, tangy smell of the marsh reminded him of the coming spring and the promise of return to Mother Nature's many blessings. The sun was setting across the wide, smooth expense of marsh grass giving a warm winter glow to natural beauty. The setting sun allowed Barringer a comfortable respite from the intense concentration of the past four hours. He drove to the hospital comfortably.

As Barringer entered the autopsy room, he was acutely aware of silence. On the raised center stainless steel table, a little girl was bathed in an array of incandescent lights from a dozen overhead lamps. She lay on her abdomen, her head cocked backwards, her arms behind her, her legs raised behind her, all peculiarly incongruent with any comfortable posture in life. No one else was in the room except McCarthy. He sat in a straight wooden chair staring at the girl.

"That you, Randy?"

"Yes, Joe."

"I'm waiting on some X-rays to return before I turn her."

Barringer said nothing.

"The ropes are over there. The gag is on the table. She had a cloth rammed down her throat. The panties have a hole in them in the perineal area. Could be the assailant forced something into either the vagina or the anus. Can't tell from the body. I've carefully protected the rope ends. Imagine you'll be sending them to the FBI."

"Yes."

"Don't know much about the girl yet, but don't see any positive evidence of a lot of physical abuse other than the ropes. Imagine she died of strangulation due to either the tying or the gag, or both."

"Joe, if he beat her severely, is there the possibility that we could tell from bruise deposits of blood at this date?"

"Yes, and I've already looked pretty carefully. We have means of detecting blood deposits beneath the skin, and I have found absolutely no suggestion of bruising except at the rope sites."

"Why in the devil would he do all this and leave her panties on?"

"That's what I'm sitting here considering. Randy, I think you have to consider that the guy who did this may just have wanted to watch."

"Jesus."

"Yeah, I know. But if it bears out, that may be all he did until he went too far."

"Doc, if he pushed that cloth down her throat, he would know that it could kill her."

"Yes, and if he pulled the feet up that high with the other end tied to her neck, he would know he was killing her."

"Do you expect the X-rays to show anything?"

"No, but I want to check broken bones and internal foreign objects before beginning a dissection. We've taken dental X-rays and are getting her X-rays from her dentist, but the gross characteristics already match and the clothes are the same as Mary Brady was wearing. It's Mary Brady, unofficially."

"Joe, I've got to get a conference going. Would you give me a ring later?"

"Sure."

"Joe, we thank you. Wouldn't know how to proceed if we didn't have you."

"Randy, first, you're welcome, but I know better than that. It's us citizens who should be thanking you for trying to prevent things like this from happening again. You take care."

"See you later."

Barringer stopped at a hallway pay phone and called home. He explained his situation, chatted for a minute, and then went to the hospital cafeteria. He frequently ate there with Jenny, and the waitresses knew him.

"What's got you here so late, Captain?"

"Oh, just having to work late. Figure I couldn't get the job done if I didn't come over here and get some of this delicious food."

Both laughed. Barringer sat away from the others and studiously reflected on his next moves. He wolfed down his sandwich and French fries and drank his coffee slowly. He watched one of the hospital employees walk past the cash register without paying. He looked intently at the cashier, but it was impossible to tell if she hadn't noticed or was part of the small swindle. *People have to be taught honesty. They don't care about it naturally*, he thought. He finished his coffee, walked close to the thief's table, snapped a mental photograph, and left.

He drove slowly and thoughtfully to the station. Psychologically he was trying to adjust to the mental discipline that the next twenty-four hours would require. Faced with the small girl on the autopsy table, it is human to want to begin the hunt, to go for the perpetrator at full speed, to re-examine every suspect in person. It is natural under the circumstances to seek vengeance. He knew better. His success had been build on restraint, on slowing down the process of emotional stimuli and providing an extremely considerate investigation. It would begin tonight with a large conference and continue tomorrow with a review of critical facts. He had arrived at the station and parked his car while still in deep contemplation.

Barringer began setting up the amphitheater. He had two large chalk boards. On one he would plot summaries of information. On the other he would begin to design the type of investigation that best fitted the available information. At each point he would stop and allow full discussion from everyone. It was a long and tedious method, but when finished, everyone had his say and all were well-informed as to the case and its next logical steps.

Years ago when he had begun this type of approach he had received little more than gentle ridicule. Later, when interest began to appear, there was argument. Now, no one wanted to be left out, and many others had adopted his style. Still, it was tiresome and very consuming. He cut on the switches to the central taping system. Every comment would be taped and later typed and distributed. The distribution had made each person aware of the value of his own discussion. Consequently the process had become much more efficient and effective.

There had been an initial problem with the press. A bargain had been made with the TV stations and newspapers. The press received improved information and consumed less energy in getting it. In trade, the police were given better security for information useful in investigations.

Randy checked on the availability of two slide projectors. McCullum would have slides already prepared. Years ago he objected to the haste of this arrangement, not wanting to be hurried. He was a perfectionist of the finished print and didn't wish to have his reputation displayed in hastily prepared slides. Barringer had bargained with him. The two men agreed on the use of machine-prepared slides for this type of conference and kept the manually produced prints for the court scenes. The bargain had caused considerable turmoil in local legal circles, but with no law transgressed, Barringer's bargain remained intact. Finally he checked on the snack bar being well-equipped to handle the crowd until late. He knew if he could keep them satisfied, he could keep their attention. It was their eyes and ears and memories that he wanted. From their standpoint, they wanted part of the action. If Barringer could provide, they would listen.

Dr. Ben Rider came in early. Barringer met him pleasantly.

"Hello, Ben. How are you?"

"Well, thank you, Randy, how about yourself?"

"Good."

"What's this about, Randy?"

"Ben, we've got a real peculiar one. If you will remember, about a year ago, two teenage girls disappeared from Pirates Beach. They've never been found. About two months ago, another girl named Mary Brady disappeared. We have found the body of Mary Brady. Joe McCarthy just called me and said the dental evidence matches. She had been bound and gagged and probably died as a result of the gagging or the binding. She does not appear to have been raped, although she may have been molested. Joe thinks that her assailant may have simply subdued her for voyeuristic purposes. Right now it's a tenable thesis. Additionally, about two weeks ago, a patrolman at Pirates Beach found three girls bound and gagged beneath some stairs to a beach house in the same vicinity. So it looks like we have a sicko loose. I need your help."

"Sure, I'll listen attentively. Maybe we can talk afterwards."

"Sure. Well, the others are arriving. How about sitting up here? You are probably going to be the most important source of information on this case."

Rider smiled to himself. He wondered how many of the others Randy would tell were the most important people here. He momentarily wondered if Randy would have made a good psychiatrist but was soon absorbed in the growing crowd of police and other talents. He knew many of them on friendly terms, had taken care of several. He nodded and smiled and settled himself to concentrate on Barringer's description of one of society's sicknesses.

The large room was half-filled with people. Most were from the law enforcement agencies. All knew that if Barringer had arranged a conference, some important event had taken place, probably a murder with a complex twist. Some had already heard and deduced much of what would be explained. For most of the lawmen, it was a chance to socialize, to trade recent political and practical information. Most knew that their departments or agencies would probably not become involved, but it was gratifying to have the inside information. Then, too, they knew Barringer was genuine in attempting to solicit all outside help possible and any information that might be helpful. The room buzzed with gossip, new stories, old rehashes. The lawmen were careful to speak to the administrators and mayors. The politicians spoke back in friendly tones. Nineteen seventy-four was an election year, and one could not have too many constituents. As eight o'clock approached they sequestered into small groups and gradually lowered the tone of their backslapping conversations.

Chief Hardy took the podium. Barringer sat near him.

"Ladies and gentlemen. We very much appreciate your presence here tonight. We were informed by my good friend Chief Gooding that they had found a young girl buried in the sand at Pirates Beach this morning. Captain Barringer and I have been investigating the site this afternoon. He will give you our findings and solicit your help and cooperation in this affair. We are grateful to you for coming tonight, and we appreciate your help."

Randy replaced the chief at the podium. He waited for the chief to be seated and stalled for a moment reviewing the notes on his legal pad. When he perceived that he had the attention of all, he began.

"Recently, a man walking his dog on Pirates Beach noticed that the dog kept sniffing an area in the dunes. The man saw a human hand, he reported it to Chief Gooding, and the chief called us. Dr. Dan Davis carefully excavated a body this afternoon, and Dr. Joe McCarthy called me officially a few minutes ago and said that he had made a positive ID as that of Mary Brady, a girl missing from Pirates Beach for the past two months. The subject was a white female, age seventeen. She had been last seen in downtown Pirates Beach by two female companions on the afternoon of February 21, 1974. She was a well-liked high school junior. There was no history of trouble, drugs, arrests, or bad companions. Her friends said that when last seen, she was happy and unworried. She did not get home after leaving the two companions. The past two months' investigation has not produced leads of significant value. Preliminary examination by Dr. McCarthy tonight suggests that she was killed by strangulation. She had been bound."

Barringer cautiously left out the gag and the type of bondage. The older lawmen noted the omission and knew the reason for it.

"So far as we can tell, she was not raped."

Barringer used the term rape instead of sexual assault intentionally. Only one or two in the audience made note of the difference. Among them was Dr. Rider.

"Possibly related to this crime is the circumstance that two girls have been missing from Pirates Beach since May 23, 1973. They are Shirley Clair and Alice Lawton, both white females ages fourteen and fifteen, and residents of Pirates Beach. Again, they were well-respected girls with no history of trouble. They too, were last seen in the afternoon while walking on the beach."

Barringer paused and looked for McCullum. He spotted him with a slide tray near the back of the room.

"Additionally, a Pirates Beach patrolman found three teenage girls bound and gagged beneath stairs to a beachfront house two weeks ago. The girls state that they were visiting Pirates Beach and had been sunbathing. A white male of dark complexion, approximately thirty years of age with dark hair and a small mustache, approached them with a gun. He told them that he had killed two police officers and would hold them as hostages. He tied and gagged the three of them beneath a beach house stairway. They were found by a Pirates Beach patrolman investigating a surfing complaint."

Most of the audience had followed accounts of each circumstance in the papers. Barringer realized their knowledge but was using the historical review to reorganize the events so that they might represent a pattern. Immediately there was a response.

"Yes, Chief Scott?"

"Randy, wasn't there a similar circumstance in your area about the same time this Brady child disappeared?"

"Yes, Chief Scott, I was going to discuss it later. On Tuesday, February 12 of this year, two weeks before Mary Brady disappeared, a fourteen-year-old white female was accosted by a twenty- to thirty-year-old dark-complexioned white male with dark hair and a mustache. He threatened her with a knife, took her into a wooded area near her home, made her undress and assume various lewd positions. He felt her up, but did not violate her. He watched her in various poses for almost a half hour, then tied her to a tree and left."

Chief Scott nodded. He was known for a superb memory and he was proud of it. Frequently he remembered so many possible related events to a case that he had to be gently avoided.

Another hand went up.

"Yes, Captain Brown?"

"Randy, since the last case you mentioned happened near a road to Pirates Beach, and the three missing persons are from Pirates Beach, and the three other girls beneath the stairs were on Pirates Beach, it's hard to avoid the assumption that your man lives on Pirates Beach."

"It's beginning to look that way."

Randy knew the comment had not arisen to express the obvious. He waited.

Brown went on.

"We busted a dealer last month from Pirates. When we got him, he had two young girls with him, one fourteen and one fifteen; both are pretty well-addicted."

Barringer glanced at Canthus. Their eyes met, Canthus nodded. Rodney Canthus was Barringer's authority on narcotics. By his barely perceptible nod, he had told Randy that he knew of the bust and the circumstances. Now he raised his right index finger near his temple as if he were brushing his hair with his hand. As one of many signals that the squad had practiced, he was informing Barringer that the subject under discussion might be a prior suspect.

"Captain Brown, was the subject indicted?"

"Yes Randy, he is still in the vicinity. We saw him day before yesterday on the east side, presumably still dealing."

"Do we know where he is staying?"

"Yes sir. I'll get with Canthus later."

"Thanks, Charlie."

"Speaking of suspects, Herb Lennon's boy is still on Pirates."

"The one who beat up those kids last year?"

"Yeah."

"I thought they put him in the tank."

"They did, but they released him during Christmas. He's on Pirates and just as mean as ever."

Barringer nodded at Fielding. Fielding was writing. He glanced back and acknowledged the information.

Another hand.

"Randy, this cat is loco. He has killed a young girl in a strange way, may have killed the others, and tied up three more, all within a few blocks of each other. It sounds like he is trying to be caught. What do the head doctors think?"

"Dr. Rider?"

Rider rose. He was thoughtful, pensive. He was a serious man, well trained in psychiatry, known to most present. He, like others, had been recruited by Barringer. As with many of Barringer's ideas, he had not been accepted at first. It was his use of well-proven facts rather than obscure theories that had won his confidence among the protectors of the law. That and hypnosis. Rider had a little of the actor in him, and his use of hypnosis when questioning suspects had allowed him a bit of the stage. He loved it. Rider's use of hypnotic anesthesia, of sticking pins in his hypnotized subjects' arm without any sign of pain fascinated the onlookers. They regarded him as a bit of the circus barker that he was. Rider was serious now.

"Gentlemen, I think from the little bit of information that I've been able to get so far, that we're faced with a real sick person, a very dangerous person."

The audience quieted.

"It may be that the assailant in this area is torturing his victims. Not torturing in the usual sense of carefully inflicting physician pain, but rather purposefully inflicting mental pain in the form of fear. It appears that he is selecting so far as we know, young girls, the kind that would be driven almost crazy with fear from the acts that this man is performing. As I was sitting here listening to Captain Barringer and trying to remember the news accounts of these happenings, I could not help but try to understand what was happening from the victim's viewpoint. In each instance, it must have been a terrifying event. Perhaps that terror is intentional, just as it is with the Middle Eastern terrorist who plants bombs in airports and that sort of thing. Perhaps the terrorist in this instance is so mad at himself or so disappointed in himself that he can only vindicate himself by terrifying someone else—preferably a small, defenseless person. If so, we're dealing with a sick person who will kill again if given time. There is probably no way he can gain enough confidence from anything to quit feeling that he must terrorize others. I would offer that this person has killed others and that his acts of killing and terror will only increase in frequency now. I feel that we should use all possible methods to find him as soon as possible."

The room was quiet. Any sense of lightness generated by a congenial gathering of men familiar to each other was gone. They were a stern group now.

For the next two hours, questions and discussions flowed freely. McCullum showed the slides of the afternoon activities. Barringer encouraged all to interact. They compared known suspects, methods of operation, recent rapes, burglaries, and numerous persons known to be of violent tendencies.

At 10:30 p.m., the chief and Barringer summed up the meeting and expressed the gratitude of his department for the cooperation of his colleagues. Most left, satisfied of their role in a community effort.

Dr. Rider remained for a moment.

"Randy."

"Yes, Ben."

"I know you've got a lot to do, but I want to leave you with a couple of thoughts."

"Sure, you know I depend on you."

"Randy, this guy is out of control. He may even want to be caught, subconsciously, you know. My point, however, is that he isn't normal. My guess is that he is full of hate. If you tumble onto him and go for him, go in force. Don't you go alone, and don't let anyone of your men try by himself. There is some sort of primitive drive in this one."

"Thanks, Ben. We'll remember, and we'll heed your advice."

"Randy, the other thing, and this is just a feeling, but I feel it pretty strongly. This guy may have killed before, maybe more than once, or even a few times. If you catch him, and you will, check his past carefully."

"We will Ben. By the way, Ben, what is your gut feeling about what is pushing this guy? What is producing his hate?"

"I don't know, Randy. Sometimes it is so inexplicable that I think it's born in some people, encased in the genetic code."

# Chapter XIII

Barringer bade Dr. Rider goodnight and walked to his office. He was beginning to feel the length of the day and the multitude of plans necessary to organize an investigation. When he arrived at his office, Margaret Barr was waiting for him. He had noticed her in the audience but had forgotten her in the many discussions that had been held. She had not wanted to interrupt his conversation with Dr. Rider and had slipped by to wait for him quietly in the office. Pierce had let her in and fixed her a cup of coffee.

Margaret Barr was every inch a lady. She was in her sixties, prim and proper, gray haired with gold rimmed spectacles. She epitomized the classical librarian. Everything about her suggested that one be quiet and subdued in her presence. She ran the county library with a firm and diligent hand. Her husband was a collector of stamps and old coins and seemed to prefer to collect them than sell them in his shop. Their most lighthearted moments seemed to be those at the ice cream parlor after a concert. Margaret Barr was as foreign to the Detriville police station as would be a hummingbird among condors. The mystery of incongruity is that it is always present, for Margaret Barr sat skimming through one of Randy Barringer's books on kidnapping as he walked through the door of his office.

"Good evening, Captain Barringer."

"Good evening, Mrs. Barr. You are very kind to have come to our meeting."

"Thank you, Captain, I am most interested in the problem. It would seem that the community can ill afford not to pursue this matter with all haste."

"Yes, Mrs. Barr, it is a profoundly disturbing situation."

"What can I do for you, Captain?"

"Mrs. Barr," Randy leaned forward in his chair trying to organize previous thoughts. "I very seriously need someone of your talent to put in order the many details taht have been uncovered today and those that have been accumulating since the first two girls have been missing. As you would expect, a series of investigations have begun, wound down, been restarted, and have culminated today. The data probably involves seven young girls, two missing, the one found today, one attacked off the Pirates Beach road, and the three found bound and gagged last week. There may be others. I need your help in much the same way as we worked the case two years ago. Could you help?"

Margaret Barr watched Barringer carefully as he talked. The situation reminded one of the old maid school teacher and her bad, but bright favorite school boy. Barringer had been involved with an extremely complex murder case two years previously, requiring an immense effort at putting complex technological information into a logical format that could be well understood by his men and a jury. Margaret Barr had watched him for several days in her library as he pored over a massive amount of chemical and physical information and busied himself with a huge note-taking task. It had been rare for her to have a police captain utilize so much of her library, and as she put the books back onto the shelves later, she could not help but wonder at the point of the study. On the third day she had asked him about his studies and had found him intelligent and capable. He had warmed to her interest and stumbled upon the possibility of having her help. He had approached the idea cautiously, no precedent being available to involve librarians in murder cases. From the first he had noted the enthusiasm, a sense of intense curiosity, and an almost glimmer of excitement. His gamble had paid off with one of the best-researched cases he had experienced. She had preferred anonymity, apparently being well-paid by having been involved in a useful effort.

Barringer saw the same glimmer of excitement now. She wanted to be part of the action again. Randy reflected on the excitement for a moment. He had been raised among ladies similar to Mrs. Barr. There were the same sorts of ladies in his childhood, the ladies of the church, the ladies of the teas, the ladies of the bridge parties, the ladies of the civic groups and the garden parties and the preservation societies. The ladies are always good, he thought, perhaps it is because they are not free enough to be bad or perhaps it is because someone has to be good to add balance to society. Perhaps it is because they are the strong ones. Men often grow weaker with age, growing beyond the point of being capable of keen competition, but the ladies only grow stronger, perhaps because they were never given the challenge to be strong in their younger lives. As he looked at Mrs. Barr, the doubts of the cause and effect of her being here was of little moment. She was organization. She was perfection in placing a detail in its proper location in time and place. She did not appear to try to impress her opinion as to the relevance of the detail or whether it was accurate or spurious, only that it be properly displayed in terms of its occurrence and its fitness. Barringer liked that. He knew that eventually he was the balance in which all data must weigh itself. He would determine what was important, possible, probable, and real. He was the cauldron of final decision. He must eventually point to the correct path of investigation, but the perfection of the job was the perfection of its organization.

Margaret Barr had listened carefully to Barringer's request for help. "Certainly, I will be glad to help. How do you wish for me to proceed?"

"You have heard the briefing. I would like for you to go back over all of the data with Pierce and the men. Let them tell you exactly what has happened today. Much of it has been left out during the conference."

"Why?"

"I want to retain information which is not known to others so that no possibility exists for its being known to the murderer. In that way we may be able to use some of it to obtain a confession and a conviction."

"I am not sure I completely understand."

"Well, let's suppose that we know that the murderer has a tattoo on his hand but prefer not to generally publicize it. He doesn't bother to cover it up or get rid of it, and we can use it in court at a time that he is not prepared to defend against the knowledge of it."

"I see. Do we have some of that type of information now?"

"Yes, a good bit from this afternoon. You will have all of it, but it stays here."

"Of course."

"It's late now, almost eleven. Are you too tired to listen to Pierce for awhile?"

"No, I'm fine, eager to get started. I'll work for a while and then be back early in the morning."

"Thank you, Mrs. Barr."

"You're very welcome, Captain."

Pierce was on his feet when Randy escorted Mrs. Barr into the outer office, and the others rose also. They remember her typed summaries from the previous case. The footnotes and the reference symbols had confused them for a while, but as they got used to the method, several of them had tried to adopt part of it into their own note-taking methods. Randy explained to the officers that Mrs. Barr would be working with them to form a repository of information as the investigation proceeded. She would act to organize incoming information and cross reference it against other similar information. The men were by nature secretive, suspicious, and competitive, but they knew that Mrs. Barr would give proper credit to the person producing the information and that if it turned out to be important, it would be written plainly for the captain to see. Each officer's ownership of information was therefore effectively protected, they were spared the tedious task of writing it all up, were not subjected to the risk of not cross-correlating it against other information, and were given an incentive to produce to benefit their own reputations. They unloaded on Mrs. Barr. They produced fresh coffee, brought her cookies from the machine, and even delegated one of themselves to go out for a glass of milk. Margaret Barr listened to each in turn, being certain of the time of events, who was present, who could corroborate, and who had similar information. She kept them directed to the events of the day. When one would occasionally slip in an irrelevant event, she would steer the conversation gently but firmly back to the investigation. They talked to each other for three hours while Mrs. Barr wrote steadily. When at two o'clock she glanced at the clock, she pretended surprise. The men were fading, and they quickly agreed to begin again in the morning.

While Margaret Barr had been interviewing the investigation team, Randy Barringer had left. He drove to the Detriville General Hospital and met again with Dr. McCarthy. The two men conferred for an hour regarding the autopsy findings on Mary Brady.

"As far as I am concerned, death occurred by strangulation, either due to having the gag shoved down over her windpipe, or the rope around her neck, or both."

"Do you have anything more regarding sexual molestation?"

"No, Randy, except that there is a hole in her panties in the area of the vagina. It could have been made by forcible entry of the fingers or of a foreign object of some sort."

"No further evidence of being battered?"

"No."

"Any specimens?" Asked Randy knowing full well that Dr. McCarthy had saved numerous ones.

"Yes, over on that table, let's go over these. On your left, in those envelopes, are samples of hair from the head and pubic region. In that first plastic bag is a piece of cloth that was tightly knotted about her upper neck. In the next bag is a similar piece of cloth more loosely tied around her lower neck. I have left the knots intact by cutting the cloths at designated areas."

"Good, I see the tags."

"In that bag are her panties. You can see the hole I was talking about."

"Yes, pretty symmetrical isn't it?"

"Yes, it's more probable that a foreign object was used than fingers. Next are the gag and a synthetic cloth such as is used for dish washing. It has a pretty distinctive design. Coiled in the next bag is the rope used to bind her. It appears to be an inexpensive syntheticm possibly of the clothesline type. Again I preserved the knots and the rope ends."

"Do you mind if I take these with me now?"

"No, go right ahead. By the way, I photographed those carefully."

"Thanks, Joe, once again you've done an excellent job. Sorry it caught you at such a bad time."

"No problem, Randy. I would appreciate your letting me know how this one goes. It's a pretty bad person who would distort a young girl to this degree." McCarthy's voice gave a little. It was barely perceptible and perhaps would not have been noticed by many. Barringer caught it, and it made him even more appreciative of the deep nature of Joe McCarthy. Perhaps, he thought, McCarthy's sensitivity was one of the factors that prompted him to be so thorough. He would try to remember that when next he became irritated with McCarthy's snail-like pace.

"Good night Joe, we appreciate your help."

"Night, Randy."

On the way out of the building Barringer called the mayor of Pirates Beach and informed him of the positive identification of Mary Brady. He was grateful that the mayor preferred to inform the parents rather than subject the police to this sensitive duty. He knew that the mayor would spend the majority of the night with the Brady family.

Barringer walked into the night and breathed deeply. The cool spring air was invigorating. He slid into the driver's seat, placed the specimens on the back seat, automatically made a visual checked of the radio channel, the dashboard gauges, and the semi-recessed weapon in the door. He started the car, listened to the sound of the powerful engine, waited for it to settle. Satisfied with the vehicle, he turned on the desk switch and wrote in his log for several minutes. Turning the light off, he radioed the dispatcher and gave her his next destination. Then he drove back to Pirates Beach.

The marsh was beautiful at night. The air was completely still. The near full moon reflected from the numerous creeks as if they were silver serpents painted on a dark grassy canvas. There were no birds at this time, no life, just the dormant power of one of nature's estuaries, concealing a tremendous quantity of sleeping fish, fowl and vegetation, all of which awaited the sunshine of tomorrow.

Barringer's automobile slowed at the grave site. Immediately a young patrolman who had been standing in the trees approached. He was holding his flashlight in his left hand. Randy noted that his service revolver was on his right hip and that the retainer strap was unbuttoned. He smiled to himself thinking of youth and its ever-present need for excitement. He let the flashlight be played across his face. Suddenly the light quickly averted.

"Excuse me, Captain, I didn't know it was you."

"That's all right. It's Johnson isn't it?"

"Yes sir, Bob Johnson, Captain."

"Is everything quiet?"

"Yes sir, a lot of curiosity seekers earlier tonight according to the early shift, but nothing much since."

"Good. Bob, I want to look around for a few minutes. I want to try to see how this place would look at night. Would you mind switching off those temporary lights for me and letting me wander about for a while?"

"No, sir. I'll be glad to. Anything you want me to do?"

"No."

Patrolman Johnson heard the "no" very clearly. It sounded like a quiet gun shot, and its meaning was obvious. Johnson walked over to the temporary pole and switched off the lights bathing the area. When his eyes had accommodated to the semi-darkness, Barringer had disappeared without a sound. For the next half hour Johnson stood beside the pole peering into the moonlit surroundings. For several minutes Barringer's form could be seen clearly beside the grave site, then he would appear to be walking backwards, then he would disappear. Suddenly the shower stall door would open, a window would shut. Next Barringer would be on the beach, then across the dunes, then back onto the beach, all without the usual sound of someone walking. Johnson was looking for Barringer intently when an arm touched his right shoulder. He automatically swung his hand toward the service revolver but the other hand had swung more quickly down his right arm staying the movement.

"Didn't mean to startle you, Johnson. Shouldn't have come up behind you like that. Sorta forgot myself while I was concentrating on my job."

Johnson was frozen. The scar on Barringer's face showed in the moonlight as if it had been sculptured to terrify others. Johnson's heart was racing. He tried to gather himself.

"It's all right, Captain, you kinda startled me. Want the lights back on?"

"Sure, and thanks a lot. Hope you have a pleasant evening."

By the time the lights came on Barringer was near his car. In a few minutes he was gone. Patrolman Johnson turned his flashlight on and nothing remained of Captain Barringer's presence. The remainder of his vigil that evening was restless. It seemed that many more odd sounds occurred afterwards than before Barringer's visit. For a month thereafter Johnson could feel Barringer's hand touch his shoulder.

It was nearly 4:00 a.m. Barringer drove home, drank a small glass of milk, turned off the light, undressed and crawled into bed. He gently touched Jenny's shoulder, felt her fingers close over his for a few seconds and then sleepily fall away. He buried his face in the pillow and slept soundly until 7:00 a.m.

# Chapter XIV

At 7:00 am the alarm clock near Barringer's head made a scratching noise. His large hand closed about the small clock just as the bell began to ring. By the time the bell chirped twice, an index finger tip found the off switch and effectively silenced one of man's worse inventions. One of his eyes opened to read the awful reality of how fast the earth turns and then he forcefully opened the other eye. He lay gazing at the sunlit yard through a crack in the blinds. He knew without turning that the other side of the bed was empty. He could not remember Jenny leaving, but knew that she would be true to her habit of arriving at the hospital at seven. He wondered for a moment how his body could sense the absence of hers. He gave up this rather mystical inquiry rather quickly, for he could now smell the bacon and eggs that she had left for him. After a shower and a satisfying cup of coffee and breakfast, he scanned the newspaper's account of yesterday's morbid events. He smiled as he recognized the familiar quotations from the chief about public safety and the excellent record of crime solution by his department. He became more serious in wondering at the nature of the impact of the story on the murderer. Finally his mind turned to the probability that the story would stimulate a rash of phone calls, tips, threats, and false alarms. He knew that the only defense for such an onslaught was reviewing all of the factual material currently available.

He was at the office by 8:00 a.m.

"Pierce?"

"Yes, sir."

"Good morning."

"Good morning, sir."

"Get along all right with Mrs. Barr last night?"

"Yes sir. Captain?"

"Yes, Pierce."

"You get along all right with Patrolman Johnson last night?"

Barringer glanced at the wide grin on Pierce's face. He smiled in as guilty a fashion as he could muster.

"Pierce."

"Yes, sir."

"I want everybody in the conference room."

"Mrs. Barr, too?"

"She here?"

"Yes, sir."

"Yes, by all means."

"I'll have 'em in there in fifteen minutes."

"And Pierce."

"Yes, sir."

"Have all material available on this case, a pot of coffee, and send someone for doughnuts on the account. We're going to be in there for a while."

"Yes, sir."

"Good morning, Captain Barringer."

"Good morning, Mrs. Barr."

"When the others come in, Captain, would you like for me to review what I've been able to piece together so far?"

"Yes, Mrs. Barr, that would be perfect."

The conference room filled quickly. The men knew from past experience that the captain would be in a business mood this morning. He would not be tolerant of tardiness, meandering, and unsubstantiated information. He would want facts in a chronological order. He would wish to begin at the first event in the case and review all relevant material to the present time. Last night's review was intended to provide the press, and consequently the pubic, with information their allowed the public their due and their ability to be helpful. This morning was designed for the organization of details in such an array as to allow insight into patterns and forms. Only in this way could subsequent information be inserted to add to the fabric of the case and not to detract or distort.

The group quickly assembled. Lieutenant Roger Pierce came in with Margaret Barr. The two had been talking for the past hour. Pierce liked Mrs. Barr because he knew that the captain liked her. If the captain thought Mrs. Barr was beneficial, then she was an important person and he could learn from her. Pierce was eager to learn. He aspired to one day wearing a captain's bar on his lapel and leading an investigative team. He had natural leadership abilities, was liked by his men, and attempted to learn at every possible opportunity. He was wise enough to know that he did not have Barringer's wide latitude of natural talents, and he substituted hard work and firm commitment. He knew by Barringer's frequency of advice that he had capability, and he was, by nature, patient enough to make use of every asset and every opportunity. Pierce was a big man, naturally powerful, but more reliant on his ability to talk to people and guide them with words than by use of a hard stick. His only aggressive moves came when there was danger approaching the captain or when one of his men was threatened.

"Mrs. Barr, we appreciate your meeting with us so early. We will listen to you and then begin to formulate a plan for further investigation.

Elizabeth Barr sat primly and properly at one end of a large oaken conference table. The table had inhabited the kitchen of the Barringer home when Randy was a small boy. It had been removed and stowed when the kitchen was renovated. When Barringer was given the investigative unit and the present offices, he had retrieved the table of his boyhood. As he now glanced across the table at Mrs. Barr, dressed in a stiff white blouse holding her graying head high and readjusting her gold rimmed glasses, it seemed to him that he had momentarily reentered a memory of thirty years previously. His nostalgic review lasted only a few seconds, however, for Mrs. Barr began to reiterate the more morbid memories of only a year ago.

"Captain Barringer, with your permission, I am going to try to provide you with an outline of events as they relate to the case at hand. I say outline, for I have not yet had sufficient time to place details in their proper perspective. You should also realize that all of the events to which I shall direct attention may or may not be actually related. The judgment as to their relationship has already been made in the past, and I simply have tried to provide these events in a proper sequence."

The men listened intently. Bartey came up out of his slouch into a sitting position. Fielding's face appeared usually serious. The room appeared to represent fourth-grade school boys waiting for the teacher to tell them about summer vacation.

Mrs. Barr looked up from her material. Barringer nodded.

Mrs. Barr began an outline of all events that were reasonably associated with the case. To one listening, it was as if ones' grandmother had come to visit and had promised to read a story. There was rapt attention and no interruption until she came to the list of suspects that Bartey had uncovered.

Barringer interrupted. "Detective Bartey, were these men ranked?"

"No, sir. We couldn't find anything to point out why any one of them might have been more guilty than any other."

"Was there a psychological profile completed?"

"Yes, sir. If you will remember, you went with me to Dr. Rider's to begin the profile. I later took each case and each suspect's general description to him."

"Did he ever complete the profile?"

Mrs. Barr spoke. "Yes, Captain, I have it here. Dr. Rider's suggestion was that a kidnapper existed on Pirates Beach. He was probably a single man, although being married with a family was not to be excluded. He was probably a pleasant, helpful, quiet type who was generally likeable. He would most probably be somewhat moody and tend to be a loner, but when he wished could be an intelligent, communicative person. He would tend to avoid conflict and argument. He probably had reason to hate his mother. He had probably been abused in some way as a child. He would be a person unlikely of being suspected of kidnapping or murdering a child. If he were intelligent, he would be hard to find because his deeds would be at random and would be unplanned."

"Did Dr. Rider say anything about what would be the driving force to initiate kidnapping or murder?"

Bartey spoke up. "He said that whoever the man was, he was probably driven by hate and anger."

"At what?"

"At anything."

Bartey's answers were quick and definite in much the same way as his own capacity for violence. Barringer watched him as he replied. Bartey was a keen interest of his, a challenge to analyze in terms of intensity.

"What do you think, Bartey?"

"I think the Doc's probably right, I believe we're dealing with a psycho who may be under our nose, but not obvious."

"What do you think triggers him?"

"I dunno, Captain. Maybe at times something inside of him just breaks loose. Maybe he wants to hurt something, maybe make somebody afraid, some sort of payback thing, maybe to his old lady."

Barringer nodded. All of the team had worked the Brady case. It had been an opportunity to test the speed of mobilizing his civilian volunteer surveillance team. Most of them were veterans and outdoorsmen, recruited a year previously but not used as a team until the Brady disappearance. They worked all weekend but most had to return to work on Monday. The action had turned up a number of interesting problems. There were more arrests for drunken driving on that weekend than any other in the year. There were more areas of acute embarrassment of males and females being where they were not supposed to be than on any other occasion. There were five cases of violation of search and seizure, six cases of accidental discovery of drug violations, two political embarrassments, two burglaries-in-progress cases, and a prevention of an abduction of a child in an unrelated situation. The news media had caught the intensity of the case and amplified it. Pirates Beach was tense. As anxieties intensified and observation sharpened, it could be noted that few children were apparent anywhere on the beach and none were without a parent.

The nearby city of Detriville did not appear disturbed. Only the police force worked tirelessly. Barringer remembered that weekend. He had involved himself beyond his usual habit. He had begun with the spot where Mary had last been seen. Her friends had told him the direction that Mary had used as she walked away. Barringer had walked in every direction that his instinct had prompted. His men were accustomed to his persistence, but even they had become impatient with him that weekend. Now as they all sat quietly reviewing the known facts, they remembered how close the captain had come to predicting what had evidently happened to Mary Brady. Now that they knew where she had been buried, they were desperately trying to forget the telephone calls to Miami, Chicago, Los Angeles. They had already succeeded in forgetting the many theories they had advanced that had proven fruitless. The human mind tends to suppress that which is injurious whether to the body or to the ego. Their focus of attention now was the hunt. It had been ascertained that a death had occurred, and the smoldering fire of doubt had been rekindled by the flames of certainty. The hunt had been restarted, and each of these men were trained for the hunt.

Bartey began again. "The disappearance of Mary Brady didn't add anything concrete to the case. It was like she disappeared in a puff of smoke. We were left with one of three situations. First, she could have run away. There is nothing to suggest her as a runaway, no big heart throbs, no movie dreams, no nothing. We discarded the runaway theory. We were left with abduction off the island and death, or death and burial on the island. We looked and couldn't find her. Now we know she was buried right under our noses."

Bartey paused and picked up another note pad. He continued. "We looked back over our suspects and got a few more. The crazies started coming out of the bushes. The kinks started flipping on each other, and while we made some other cases, nothing really showed up on the Brady case. It all cooled down until last Friday."

"Okay then, maybe we're going a little fast, but what happened Friday?"

Mrs. Barr shuffled her papers and began again. "Last Friday afternoon at 3:00 p.m., Patrolman Richard Owens of Pirates Beach Police Department answered a call to the 1000 block of Atlantic Street to investigate a reported surfing problem. He parked his vehicle at 1008 Atlantic where there is a good view of the surf. As he passed the steps of 1008, he glanced down to see three young girls bound and gagged beneath the stairs. Their ankles were bound securely and their wrists were bound behind their backs. All were clothed, but all three were writhing about in the sand, obviously terrified."

Barringer considered the circumstances: that of the hundreds of beach front houses and cottages on Pirates Beach, Patrolman Owens had parked at the one house where young girls had apparently just been bound. He had been called by a citizen because of a surfing violation. Surfing violations are rare, citizen calls about surfing are rare, and the happenstance of the one house where a possible murder was being contemplated was almost too rare to believe. And yet it happened. Patrolman Owens is well-known and respected. The citizen caller was identified, and the surfers admitted they were out of their legal zone. Furthermore, one of them remembered the girls playing on the beach. It was too impossible a coincidence to occur, and yet it did. The true statistical significance of coincidence is yet to be fully explained, thought Barringer, as Mrs. Barr continues.

"Patrolman Owens immediately untied the girls. They were all essentially hysterical, so he took all of them to the house of one of their parents where they were staying. He immediately notified Chief Gooding, who then called us. Detective Bartey handled the initial events." Mrs. Barr stopped and looked at Bartey even though she knew the captain had been notified at the same time.

Bartey took up the report. "The girls were Vicky Kinnon, Nancy Farrington, and Donna Richardson, all of Sommerton. All are white, fourteen years of age and good friends. They were staying at the Kinnon cottage with Vicky's parents for the day. They had walked out on the beach after lunch, had taken a walk eastward and were returning to where they had left their towels. At approximately 3:05 p.m., as they neared 1008 Atlantic, a white male subject, approximately thirty years of age, five feet eleven inches, one hundred and eighty pounds, with dark brown hair and moustache, dressed in yellow and green frayed shorts, no shirt, wearing ankle-type tennis shoes minus shoe laces, apprehended them. He was carrying a gold colored beach towel that hid a long barreled blue revolver. He told them he had just killed two police officers and threatened to kill them if they disobeyed him.

"He forced all three girls to beneath the stairs at 1008 Atlantic where he bound them with a clothesline and gagged them with pieces of a yellow colored cloth. At about the time that he was finishing tying the third girl, he heard a car nearby and forced them to lie down beneath the stairs. The girls say that he knelt down beside one of them and appeared to be listening to the sound of the car, which kept its motor running. Apparently he got nervous and left quickly around the side of the house opposite to where you could hear the car running. Next thing they knew they were being untied by Patrolman Owens." Bartey stopped and looked at the captain.

Barringer nodded to him and said, "Go ahead with any details that you think are important."

Bartey continued, "Well, it seems that the girls are pretty consistent. All agree pretty closely on the height and weight. They are estimating age. I don't trust fourteen-year-olds' opinions of age—could have been twenty to thirty for all I know. Each one agrees about the hair and moustache. They get a little fuzzy about the shape of the face but agree as to a sort of olive-colored complexion, good teeth, smooth face, a little chest hair, not too muscular, slightly heavy. All say his eyes are the striking feature—real black, intense, scary. Each one said that his eyes and his stare made them feel afraid. Two of them told me it was as if he hated them personally and wanted them to feel afraid. All of them say they never have felt more terror. Each has stated that there was no doubt that he was going to hurt them, perhaps sexually molest them and maybe kill them. All are having intense counseling. One of the girls told me that he had a round scar on the outer part of his right lower leg. When I then asked the other two if he had any scars, one of the others corroborated it. The scar is about here," Bartey indicated the midpoint of the outer portion of his right lower leg, "and apparently the size of a quarter." Bartey stopped and looked at the captain.

Barringer said, "What is there to indicate any connection with the other girls?"

Bartey carefully separated a folder from his other notes and consulted a sheet within it. He continued, "Pirates Beach, young girls, abduction, bondage, gagging. The physical description is almost identical to that given by Carrie. The intensity, the apparent hate, the overpowering attempt to stimulate fear, all seem extremely similar. You can almost feel that it is the same guy, and from my standpoint, it seems he's getting out of control."

Barringer listened carefully. He wondered how Bartey could sense the thinking of the abductor-killer and knew that he probably could. Maybe it was that basically both of them were hunters. Different types, but hunters none-the-less.

Barringer opened his briefcase. He took from it two folders, opening one and for a few moments rearranged the paper within it.

"Let's summarize. Eleven months ago, two teenage girls disappear from Pirates Beach. By all probabilities, they are dead. Three months ago, a teenage girl is assaulted five miles from Pirates Beach. A week later another teenage girl disappears from Pirates Beach. Last week we find three teenage girls bound and gagged on Pirates Beach. Their description matches the one by the assaulted girl. Yesterday we find the body of the last missing girl, bound and gagged and sexually assaulted in a weird way. The man who had done all this is under our noses and his going to commit again. He is twenty to thirty years of age, dark skinned, maybe still has his long curly hair and moustache, and has a round scar on his right leg. He probably lives on the island. He is stepping up his activities and may be out of control. I want you to get your things together, be sure to have good radio contact, and be prepared to stay out until we've got this guy. We are not coming back in until we do, unless something else gets completely out of control. The lieutenant will stay with me. Fielding will take the business district. Go house to house first. Redo every house that's already been done. Insist on seeing every young adult male and make meticulous notes so that they can be checked. Ivers, you correlate all physical evidence and begin an approach based on physical evidence, the clotheslines, foot prints, gag material, etc. Go wherever it takes you. Bill, you and Mrs. Barr reassemble the structure of the case and analyze for anything with common denominators. Look carefully at the location, travel patterns, escape routes, etc. Try to coalesce all of our known and proven facts and rule out highly improbable parts of this puzzle."

Barringer glanced at the clock. It was 10:30 in the morning. The door to the room opened. Sarah Benton, the dispatcher supervisor, leaned through the door. "Captain Barringer, sorry to

interrupt, but a call has come in for you and it seems important."
Barringer looked at Sarah. She was an expert at the subtle art of police
communication. Barringer went into his office, flipped the recording
switches, pulled a pad to the center of his desk, readied a pen, and
picked up the telephone.

# Chapter XV

"Captain Barringer?"

"Yes."

"This is Lieutenant Shatner, Naval Base Police."

"Yes, sir."

"About thirty minutes ago a young lady called me about a problem she had last year which is similar to the ones occurring recently on Pirates Beach. May I review it with you?"

"Certainly. If you don't mind, I'll tape this."

"Sure."

"Would you start with some identifying information, and I won't interrupt you."

"I understand. This is Lieutenant Robert Shatner calling Captain Barringer. I am reporting a telephone call by Dori Weatherby to me made at approximately 10:00 p.m. today. Miss Weatherby called to report her statement made in September, 1973. At that time, she recognized a man named Albert Borgni, who she stated had assaulted her. At that time she was advised to make the statement to the Pirates Beach Police but apparently she decided not to. On reading of similar attacks on others and the recovery of a young girl's body last week, she had called to remind us of the incident that happened to her. She has stated, and we have a copy of her written statement, that she was assaulted on Pirates Beach on September 19, 1973. Her assailant forced her at gun point to a vacant house on Pirates Beach and attempted to rape her. He was unsuccessful.

"About two weeks later she recognized her assailant in the Oak Lounge at the Naval Base and informed the Naval Police. We apprehended Albert Borgni and questioned him. He is a sailor aboard the USS Sandpiper and denied the allegations. We advised Miss Weatherby to make a report to the civilian magistrate but apparently she never did, and Borgni was never formally charged with a civilian felony. We had no charge and released him. Miss Weatherby is willing to pursue the matter now because she realizes that Borgni could be involved with other girls and may have killed the child found last Wednesday. We have checked on Borgni. He is living on Pirates Beach at 903 Atlantic with his wife and two children. He has a bunk and locker aboard the Sandpiper. Figured I better call you."

Barringer knew what he had. He was busily trying to decide the next best step.

"Lieutenant, do you know if Borgni is aboard the Sandpiper now?"

"We checked that. He is off today and tomorrow."

"What do you think about looking at his room?"

"No sweat, we had expected that you would want to."

"How about now?"

"Good enough, we'll wait here at the station for you."

Barringer put the phone down. He took a deep breath and made some notes on the pad in front of him. He then turned the page and began listing steps to be taken in the further investigation of Borgni. He turned another page and listed steps to be taken if any evidence could be obtained that indicated that Borgni was a murderer. Barringer picked up the telephone. He dialed the Navy Base number.

"U. S. Naval Base."

"Yes, Naval Police please."

"Naval Police."

"Lieutenant Shatner, please."

"Shatner."

"Lieutenant, Randy Barringer again."

"Yes, sir."

"Would you please obtain Borgni's medical file for me and have it available when we get there?"

"Yes, sir," answered Shatner and put the phone down. He had heard that Captain Barringer was a bit peculiar.

Barringer then walked back into the squad room.

"Fielding, you and Canthus go find Magistrate Smoak. Make sure he is available for a possible search warrant. Ivers, you and Smith stay tight for an interview here at the station. Ivers, tell 75 that we may need a line up early this afternoon and that I don't want a delay with it if we need to go."

The men were scribbling their various tasks. They knew the captain had something, but it wasn't their place to question yet. A sense of the chase stirred through the group. It seemed the hunt was on.

"Pierce, you and Bartey come with me. Mrs. Barr, we may have something. Would it be possible for you to remain for a while?"

"Certainly, Captain." At that moment Mrs. Barr knew that her "boys" were closing the trap. She could never tell them that she would have loved to be in the car with them, to see the events, instead of always just reading them and filing and re-filing. But she was a lady and knew the responsibilities of being a lady and the never-ending necessity of not showing emotion.

Barringer, Pierce and Bartey drove quickly to the Naval Base. The car was unmarked, and their identifications were necessary to get them through the main gate. When they arrived at the Naval Police Station, Lieutenant Shatner was waiting for them. He introduced Lieutenant Yancy, executive officer of the USS Sandpiper. They briefly discussed the necessity of the search of Borgni's room aboard the Sandpiper. Yancy did not volunteer information on Borgni. He was caught between loyalty to one of his crew and the Navy's responsibility to cooperate with local law enforcement.

Lieutenant Shatner stated that the medical file had been sent for but would probably be fifteen to twenty minutes in arriving. The decision was made to begin the search. Using their car and following Lieutenants Shatner and Yancy, the group rode to Pier September where the Sandpiper was moored. As expected, all eyes were on the group as they boarded the vessel, and Barringer noted that heads began popping out of gangways within minutes. He mused that no set of civilian clothes had ever been developed that totally concealed the appearance of law officers on a manhunt.

They dodged overhanging hoses and pipes. They slid down steep ladders and bent through iron hatches. They clanged through steel passageways. They finally arrived at large, gray, iron room. All of the beds were identical—firm, gray, uncomfortable, cold.

"That's his rack over there. The locker at the foot of the bed is his. It's locked but this master key will fit." Borgni's locker contained, among his other personal positions, one hundred loose pages of nude women, six books of pictures of nude people in bondage, and two newspapers containing pictures of nude people in bondage.

Whey they got back to the Naval Police Station, the medical records had arrived. The physical examination had recorded a round scar on the outer portion of Albert Borgni's right lower leg.

Barringer thanked Shatner and Yancy and radioed Fielding to obtain a search warrant of Albert Borgni's Pirates Beach house. He gave as reason "to gain physical evidence to support suspicion of murder." As Fielding took the search warrant from Magistrate Smoak, he felt for his gun and adjusted it slightly forward on his hip. Canthus simply stretched his arms slightly. Bartey seemed relaxed, his eyes closed as if meditating. They all then drove to Pirates Beach, Pierce, Fielding and Canthus in one car, Barringer and Bartey in another. After discussion with Barringer, Fielding and Canthus drove to the back of Albert Borgni's house. They walked across his back yard, Fielding positioned in the yard and Canthus perched on the back porch, silently.

Barringer walked up Borgni's front steps flanked by Pierce and Bartey. Once on the front porch, Bartey stationed himself several yards to the right, capable of watching the front door or as an option going through a front porch window. Pierce was to Barringer's left, his large .45 caliber automatic in his left hand, out of sight but instantly ready for use.

A man came to the door. He had dark brown hair, no moustache, had an olive-colored complexion, was approximately five feet ten inches in height, was about one hundred and eighty pounds in weight. He was lightly dressed in blue jeans, a dark blue shirt and wore open tennis shoes. His eyes were intensely dark, and they looked directly at Barringer almost appearing not to see Pierce.

"Yes?"

"Are you Albert Borgni?"

With a slight hesitation but no alteration of the intent gaze, Borgni answered "Yes."

Before the sound had stopped, Barringer's left hand had grasped Borgni's left shirt front. The hand had moved as if already programmed, not waiting to discuss between a yes and no answer. When the hand had reached the shirt, it had secured it and, within it, the entire chest and much of the arms of Albert Borgni. The hand and arm of Barringer then pulled Borgni forward and spun him firmly into the bracing of the doorway. Barringer's right hand then grasped Borgni's right wrist and brought it behind him. As Borgni's right arm came behind him, a handcuff wielded by Bartey closed on it. Barringer's left hand had released the shirt and now forced Borgni's left arm backward. Bartey's handcuffs closed again. He was quickly searched for weapons.

"You are under arrest for assault. We shall discuss the rest of what we know about you shortly. Are there any other people in this house?"

Borgni had known that the end had come the instant that he saw Barringer. "No."

They quickly read him his rights.

I. That I had the absolute right to remain silent and do not have to answer any questions or give a statement, and this fact cannot be used against me.

II. That if I do answer questions or give a statement, anything I say can, and will, be used against me in a Court of Law.

III. That I have the right to consult with a lawyer of my choice before I answer questions or give a statement and also to have him present while I am being questioned.

IV. That if I wish to talk to a lawyer or have him present, but am unable to afford to hire a lawyer, one will be appointed to represent me free of charge.

V. That if I decide to answer questions or give a statement without have a lawyer present representing me, I have the absolute right during this interview to stop answering questions and to remain silent. I fully understand each of these rights which have been explained to me, and having these in mind, I wish to waive these rights and answer questions concerning the charge of MURDER, which I have been accused of committing. No threats, force or promises of any kind have been made to me by anyone to induce or cause me to waive these rights and answer questions.

As the rights were recited he seemed to deflate, becoming smaller. Perhaps in that instant some of the evil within him flew away, unseen. He did not sigh with relief, but his head did fall forward. He asked to be allowed to sit down. Bartey took him past the rather comfortable appearing sofa to a firm, straight-backed chair. As Bartey sat Borgni down, he looked fully into his face. It was Borgni's eyes that fell, defeated. With Bartey almost too close to Borgni, the others searched the house. They found a black leather jacket, a pair of white tennis shoes, a pair of white, yellow, and green cut off plain shorts, a plastic and metal replica of a western revolver, a length of rope, black leather boots, a blue windbreaker, a six-inch piece of wood shaped as a rounded dowel, several lengths of clothesline, and a length of brown electric cord. On instructions from Barringer as each incriminating article was found and placed in its separate plastic bag, it was intentionally paraded by Borgni on the way to placement in the trunk of Barringer's car.

No one spoke to Borgni. When the search was completed, he was put in the back of Barringer's car by Bartey who sat with him. They went back to the station and placed Borgni at a wooden table in the interview room. While the others, including Mrs. Barr, watched through a one way mirror from an adjoining room, Barringer sat across the table from Albert Borgni. Bartey remained by Borgni's side. A hidden camera taped the interview and two hidden microphones recorded the audio on high fidelity tape.

"Mr. Borgni, the man who is sitting by you is named Bartey. He doesn't like you. I would prefer that you talked to me and in so doing explain fully and in detail the events that have brought us together. Give details of the first situation and, then, in chronological order, describe the other situations, all of them. Do not leave anything out because I will then be required to begin questioning you and you will not like that. Also I might tire of this and leave you with him. You may begin."

"Begin with what?"

"Mr. Borgni, do not try my patience. We are discussing young girls and murder. We already have everything we need. Your cooperation is the only thing you have now to keep you from being electrocuted by high-voltage current in front of the press and your family."

"May I have these handcuffs off?"

"Take his cuffs off."

"May I have a cigarette?"

"Give him a cigarette."

Bartey did not smoke, but this had been foreseen and cigarettes were available. Bartey lit Borgni's cigarette.

Both knew Borgni was deciding. He looked down at the table. Slowly his head rose.

"Since I was six years old..."

# Chapter XVI

"Since I was six years old I have pictures in my mind of tying other people up in different positions. As I got older, even before puberty, I sought out and found pictures of people bound and gagged and some of them being beaten and some being sexually abused. I did not know until after puberty what it all meant, but I do know that it was fascinating to me."

"Did you actually harm anyone during those years?"

"No."

"Where were you when you married?"

"In Massachusetts."

"Did you perform any of this stuff with your wife?"

"Yes, she became aware of my problem when she found a lot of written and photographic material that I had hidden at the house."

"How did she react?"

"We talked it out and she let me bind her and use her sexually, but it didn't work out, so we quit."

"All right, we'll go backwards later. You know that we have found three dead girls. Tell us about the two that you killed a year ago."

"Two years ago, I became stationed in Detriville with the Navy. My second wife (my first wife and I had been divorced) and our two children rent the house where you found me yesterday. Sometime during the month of May, 1973, I was walking on the beach in the vicinity of the 900 block. It was late afternoon, and I saw two girls playing on the beach. When I saw them, I knew I was caught up in one of my spells. I watched them for about five minutes, and the spell got worse. I could see them naked, bound, and gagged. I could actually see the bindings and how they were wrapped and knotted. I could see the fear in their faces, and I could feel how helpless they would be. I could feel their bodies and knew it would stimulate terror. While my body and mind were under absolute control, I knew what my actions had to be. I went back to my house, got some strong cloth strips, my kid's toy gun and went back to the beach. They were still there. I stood and watched them again fantasizing how they would look and walked over just as they were leaving. I pointed the gun at them, told them I had just robbed a store, that the police were looking for me, that they were my hostages and if they didn't do exactly as I told them, that I would shoot them."

"Where did you take them?"

"The same house where you found the other girl. There is a downstairs shower room with an open door."

"What did you do then?"

"I used the cloth strips to bind their wrists behind their back and also tied their ankles."

"Did you gag them?"

"Yes."

"Then what did you do?"

"I stood there watching them for a few minutes and then untied their hands and made them take off their blouses, bras, and shorts. Then I retied their hands."

"Why didn't you get them to take off their panties?"

"Because I could run my hand under their panties into their assholes and vaginas, and it terrified them more than if they were completely naked."

"Did you do this to both of them?"

"Yeah."

"What else did you do?"

"There was a chair in the shower and I sat in it and made them get into various positions and just watched them. My spell got worse and worse. I became sexually aroused but didn't rape them. When my spell got really bad I made them stand on the chair and tied their necks to plumbing pipes. While they were on the chair I kept feeling them up until they got so terrified that they knocked the chair over. They kicked around for a few minutes but then became still. I felt like cutting them down but my spell wouldn't let me. After they stopped moving, I went over and shook them, but I didn't get any response. I went over to my house to get a shovel, but when I couldn't find one, I went back and dug a grave with a shingle. I put both bodies in the grave, and I think I buried their clothes nearby, but I don't remember exactly where. I threw the shingle away."

"When was the next time you had anything to do with girls?"

Borgni shifted uneasily in his chair. He seemed to be trying to adjust his thoughts to best advantage.

Barringer had watched this hundreds of times.

"Answer me." The words were like a gunshot.

"I didn't have anything to do with any other girls until September of 1973. It was in the early afternoon and I was again walking on the beach and I saw this girl sunbathing. She was older than the first two and was well built. She seemed to be asleep, and I looked at her from several positions. She looked like she would be perfect in bondage. I would tie her differently and be more sexual with her. The spell was back and I was getting more excited. I went back to the house, cut some strips of clothesline, got some cloth strips for a gag, picked up the same toy gun and went back to the beach. She was asleep and nobody was around. I pushed the gun into the back of her neck, told her I had robbed a store, shot the guy in the store and that if she didn't do what I told her, I would shoot her, too.

"I made her gather up her things and took her to the same beach house where I killed the two other girls, but we went into another portion of the downstairs which was unlocked. I made her lie down on the couch and tied her hands and feet behind her, and gagged her. I stood there and watched her for a while. I stood her up and took her shorts off and blindfolded her. I put her in various poses, and rubbed my hands all over her body and just looked at her for a while. After watching her for a few minutes, I asked her if she would agree to have her bathing suit removed and she said she would, so I untied her feet and took her bathing suit off her, this left her nude. She told me if I would untie her she would make love to me, but I told her no. I took my pants off and kind of embraced her and rubbed against her, for a little while, but I neither had an erection or reached a climax. I did this to show her that she was completely helpless and I could do anything I wanted and she could do nothing about it. I dressed and I left the house after telling her to remain there for a few minutes. Afterwards I left and went home."

Borgni slouched. "Could I have some water?"

Barringer nodded and Bartey poured water into a paper cup from a pitcher that they had brought for just this expectation. Barringer let him have his drink of water and waited for a few seconds. He knew that once started, Borgni would purge himself, at least until he had recovered enough to plan.

"Okay, we've got a long way to go. What happened next?"

Borgni began again. "One day in February, 1974, I stopped by the Pirates Beach Shopping Center to buy some cigars. I had bought the cigars and had just gotten back in my car when I saw this girl who I assume was walking home from school, because she had books with her. I once again had mental pictures forming in my mind, this time of what she would look like tied up. I felt an overpowering urge to fantasize with this girl; I saw her turn down behind the shopping center, so I got out of my car and ran to the Blue & White store. I went inside and bought a small, sharp knife, and ran back out to the back of the shopping center. I saw the girl walking down a dirt road through a wooded area behind the shopping center. I approached her from the rear and placed the dull edge side of the knife against her throat. I told her that I had just committed a crime, that the police were looking for me, and I needed her for a hostage. She started to cry, and I told her to shut up and she did. We left the dirt road and went into the woods. I made her remove her outer garments and her panty hose, which left her in bra and panties. I cut the stockings up into strips and bound and gagged her. I felt her up a little, but mainly I just watched her. I watched her in various poses for a while, then I finally tied her by the neck with her slacks to a tree limb. I watched her awhile longer and then left her tied to the tree and went home. I knew she was tied loosely and could escape."

"If you had her in such a helpless condition why didn't you harm her like you did the others?" Barringer looked at Bartey who was watching Borgni closely.

"A car came by real close. It broke the spell. I knew I had to get out of there."

"All right, Borgni, you've left out another murder, better get to it, now."

"My next experience with fantasizing came a week or two later. I was in downtown Pirates Beach to get some cigars from the drug store. Across the street I saw a young girl talking with some of her friends. Again mental pictures began forming in my mind, this time of what she would look like tied in various poses. I felt an overpowering urge to fantasize with this young girl. I then went to my house and got the toy gun and some clothesline and returned to the downtown area. I parked my car so I could watch her and saw forming mental pictures in my mind of her various poses. I saw her leave the group and began walking down the street by herself. I walked up to her, pointed the gun at her, and told her not to move or make any noise, that I had just robbed a bar and shot the owner, and if she made any noise, I would shoot her, too. I took her to the same house that I had taken the other girls to, and we went into the downstairs room with the couch. I bound her hands and feet and gagged her with part of a bedspread I found in the house. I watched her for a while and then told her to take her clothes off. I untied her hands and she removed all of her clothing except her underpants. I made her assume various poses and rubbed my hands all over her body. When I rubbed my hands over her, it was to show her that she was powerless to resist me. I wanted to see her in a tied position, so I tied a piece of clothesline around her feet and tied the other end around her neck, with her feet behind her. She struggled and squirmed around and made some funny sounds, but I told her to relax and she quit moving. She never moved again after that. I moved her into various positions, like on her side, and I realized she wasn't moving any more. I shook her and tried to get her to talk, and I finally realized she was probably dead. I was in a daze and didn't know exactly what to do. I finally decided that I would bury her. I went back to my house and got a shovel and then returned to the beach house. I went out on the beach near the house and dug a hole and put the girl's clothing and body in the hole. I haven't attempted to fantasize with any other females. It was night time and I decided to take a walk out on the beach. I was out on the beach and there was a bonfire going, but I didn't see anybody else around. There were a pair of girl's shoes near the fire and I figured somebody might come get them. I immediately went back to my house and got the same toy gun and went back to where the girl was. I approached her with the gun and told her not to do anything, she turned around and looked at me and the gun, and started running. I just let her go and went back home."

"Borgni, you're not telling us about all the girls you've had contact with."

Borgni looked at Barringer but didn't hesitate. "The next day I went out on the beach and was swimming and getting a little sun, and I saw these three girls walking on the beach and these pictures started forming in my mind. I went home, got the toy gun and some clothesline. I stopped by the vacant beach house and got some more of the same bedspread strips that I had previously used. I approached the girls, showed them the gun and told them I had just committed a robbery and had to shoot two policemen. I told them to be quiet and do what I told them and they would be all right. I walked them a little ways down the beach and then took them up under a beach house. I tried to resist the urge to tie them up, but I felt it would be safer to do it. I made them lie down under the steps and tied their hands and feet behind them, which left them lying on their faces. I watched them for fifteen or twenty minutes and imagined them in different positions. I was trying to decide what to do with them when I heard a car pull up. When I say trying to decide what to do with them, I meant whether to just let them go or just loosen their bonds. But before I could decide this the car pulled up, so I just left and went home."

After the confession was signed and witnessed by Bartey and Barringer, the captain asked Bartey to wait outside the interview room. Bartey left, but once outside the room, turned to watch through the one way mirror to which the rest of the team was already glued.

As they watched, Barringer slowly got up from his chair and walked over to an instrument box. He flipped several toggle switches, walked back to the table opposite Borgni and sat down. He slowly unbuttoned his shirt cuffs and rolled his shirt sleeves onto his forearms. The arms were muscular. Barringer's left wrist was bound by a steel watch in a heavy leather band. It did not ordinarily show beneath the sleeve cuff but now accentuated the hardness of the left arm. Across the back of the mid portion of Barringer's left forearm was a six-inch clean straight scar. The scar required no imagination to give the impression that at sometime in the past a knife had been held away by the raised forearm. Nothing was apparent to suggest what might have happened to the person with the knife but when one's natural attention drifted from the forearm scar to the one on Barringer's cheek, a distinct feeling of uneasiness could be felt.

Borgni had that reaction. He had confessed. What did the big police captain want now? Why did he cut off the electrical switches? Why so quiet? Borgni became extremely apprehensive. Minutes had passed and the captain had not spoken. Finally, the silence ended, but as it did so, the air became charged with tension. The captain's voice was different now. It was slow and deliberate, low and purposeful.

"Mr. Borgni, I have no time to spend with you. I want to put an end to all of this. I want to clean it up, to write it up and file it. That is my job. My job is to put an end to this business. It is of no concern to me as to how it must be done. It only matters to me that you are going to finish all of the details. Do you understand me?"

Barringer had cut off the intercom. The men could not hear him but they knew by intuition what he was saying. They knew that the captain would not use an empty threat, but they knew that he would talk to Borgni in terms that Borgni could feel physically as well as hear. More than his voice, his body seemed to intimidate Borgni. While seated across a table, the physical presence of Barringer seemed to dominate the room. His head was forward and slightly at an angle. At that angle the overhead light ricocheted off the blanched facial scar.

"Are you telling me that you killed the two girls in the shower stall of the same house where we found the girl yesterday?"

Borgni moved restlessly.

"Answer me." Barringer's voice was flat but sharp.

"Yes, sir."

"Are the two girls buried nearby?"

"Yes, sir."

"Over near the next house?"

"Yes sir."

"I am going to take you out there in a little while. You are going to show me exactly where you buried them." Barringer was intent now, and the intensity was obvious. His muscles were set. His jaw clenched between words, and the words themselves were expelled sharply as if being fired from a gun. Borgni felt confined. He began to show a thin layer of perspiration. He did not realize that two of the switches thrown by Barringer cut off the air cooling coils and the air volume flowing through the small interview room.

"How many other girls have you killed in the Detriville area?"

"I haven't killed anybody else."

Barringer waited.

"I swear it, I haven't killed anybody else."

"Where else?"

"Nobody."

"Like hell."

Barringer waited.

"I had some trouble up north."

"I know about that," Barringer lied, "but that's not what I'm asking you."

"I'll swear I've told you everything about here."

Barringer waited.

"There is nothing more."

Perhaps it was the voice, perhaps the portrait of depression, the picture of an imploded person, weak now, indefinite, afraid.

Whatever the cues were, Barringer apparently made his decision. He rose, looked around at the mirrored window as if being able to see through it at the men on the other side. He frowned slightly, and the men jumped backwards trying to assume natural poses of indifference. If they had been asked, they would have known that the captain couldn't see through the one way mirror. But it seemed like he could, and he was unusual.

He opened the door to the interview room leaving Borgni practically slumped over the table.

"Let's go to Pirates Beach."

Pierce was standing by. He quietly asked, "Do you want some lunch first?"

"No, thank you. Maybe on the way. Let's get this done."

"How do you want it done?"

"He's going to show us where the other girls are. Get the same crew as yesterday."

"Lanny Brooks and the dozer?"

"No, not yet."

"Dr. David?"

"Yes, if he's up to it."

"McCullum?"

"Yes, we'll need photos as we uncover. He's got enough of the scene."

"Dr. McCarthy?"

"Yes."

"Captain, the press is around."

"Yes, I know, I'm going to the chief's office now and we'll let him handle it."

Pierce began writing in his handbook. He had learned to prepare in a manner so as not to forget one detail. As he turned to his note pad, Barringer paused and turned.

"Pierce, may I have Bartey?"

"Yes, sir."

"Have him wait with Borgni. You and the men get lunch. We'll grab a sandwich on the way out."

"How about him?" Pierce asked, pointing a thumb in Borgni's direction.

"I'll take care of him, Probably not much of an appetite. His turn to sweat, you know."

"Yes, sir. Saw you cut off the air conditioner."

"H'mmm," said Barringer as he walked towards the chief's office.

Thirty minutes later Barringer and Bartey put Albert Borgni in the back of Barringer's automobile. His wrists were shackled in stainless steel handcuffs. His head was down, pensively. When asked if he wanted a sandwich on the way, he declined. They bought him a soft drink and released his cuffs. He drank slowly as the two policemen ate their sandwiches. They were parked adjacent to a small sandwich shop, and several people had watched the two plainclothesmen take the handcuffs from the third man and give him the bottled drink. They assumed the two to be policemen, since one of them had a pistol holstered tightly over his back pants pocket and the other was too big and fierce-looking to doubt. They glanced again when the younger man reached into the back seat, pulled the third man out, took his unfinished drink away and re-handcuffed him. Finally, they drove away across the causeway, leading to Pirates Beach. Strange times, thought the observers. Wonder if it had anything to do with those murders and disappearances of the young girls on Pirates Beach?

As the three men sped across the causeway, a kingfisher banked to a complete halt in midair, his blue topnotch brilliant in the sunlight. He had been following a school of minnows in the muddy creek near the highway. His attention had been fractured by an inordinate splash further down the creek, and he used his aeronautical engineering to hang suspended, flapping his wings to exactly the rate needed not to move up, down or sideways. At this instant the unmarked police car flashed by below. The kingfisher looked directly into the face of a large man with a scar on his cheek. The man was watching him intently. The two looked at each other for a fleeting moment. The man smiled, and the kingfisher turned to his right and plummeted toward the creek, smiling.

Bartey drove to 908 Adams Street. He took Borgni from the backseat, and they walked with Barringer toward the dunes. The three men stopped near the end of the boardwalk. It was impossible to neglect the large open hole where Mary Brady's body had been removed yesterday. Borgni's attention appeared riveted on the spot.

"Remember what I told you. I want to finish this." Barringer's tone was harsh. Bartey realized that he was keeping the pressure on until he had the other grave site.

To Borgni, however, the tone was menacing, authoritative, and unforgiving. Under that atmosphere, Borgni wanted it all over. He pointed to a spot forty feet away. "Over there."

"Are you sure?"

"Yes, sir."

"Why."

"I'll never forget."

"Why did you carry the bodies so far from the shower stall?"

"Because you can't be seen from here."

Barringer relaxed. Bartey noticed it. The two men looked at each other, and Barringer nodded in a barely perceptible manner. Bartey knew he had already guessed the site, probably yesterday. It fitted, and he saw it immediately. They took Borgni back to the Detriville jail cell.

That afternoon they uncovered Alice Lawton and Shirley Clair. The twisted remains of the two young girls wrenched the hearts of the hardened policemen. Many had daughters. Most of them had interacted with the girls' parents and had felt the anguish of people whose most precious loves had been torn from them in a manner unknown until this sad afternoon.

A crowd had gathered, but there was complete silence. Each person knew they were witnessing an act so horrid as to almost be unimaginable. When it became apparent that the children had been almost naked and had been bound and gagged, a palpable tremor went through the crowd. No one spoke, but there were tears in every eye, even in the tough policemen. The children had been missing for a year and there they were, buried in a shallow grave, their bodies distorted by their bonds, their faces partially hidden by cloths tightly wrapped around their faces and necks. Even later, in their houses, they could not discuss it. All had seen horror, and none slept well that night.

The bodies were lifted from Pirates Beach at dusk. The wind had increased. The Palmetto fronds crackled in an eerie fashion. The sky was dark gray, a funeral sky, a sky saddened like the people it covered. Suddenly, the shower door slammed, causing all to turn quickly. It had only been the wind but it produced a shudder in the crowd. As tools and equipment were packed, darkness arrived and with it a distinct chill. An older generation would say it was the cold breath of the long, gone pirate men. Pirates Beach had given up the two girls, and it wailed and moaned at their loss. The beach felt unwelcome and hostile, bidding all to go home and grieve silently.

Barringer and Bartey were the last to leave, and even they did not speak. Death is tangible and that evening on Pirates Beach it touched all.

# Chapter XVII

In the interval between the arrest of Albert Borgni and his trial, Detective Bill Smith and Mrs. Margaret Barr carefully arranged the information. As quickly as Mrs. Barr had properly filed one issue, another would be brought to her by Smith.

Two days after the arrest and the public announcement of the findings of the Claire and Lawton children, Jane Hart came into the police station. She was interviewed by Detectives Bartey and Smith. Jane was a very pleasant sixteen-year-old white female who stated that she had come to Detriville to visit her uncle, Saul Weathers. While in Detriville, she was invited to a party with her cousin, Steve Weathers, on April 11, 1974. The party was located at a beach house belonging to Thomas Baughman. Ms. Hart further stated that at about 9:30 p.m. she left the beach house to walk down to the beach where they had made a bonfire. She stated that she had left her shoes beside the fire earlier. As she was stepping into her shoes, she felt as if someone was behind her. She turned and saw a man approximately five feet away hold some rope in one hand and a small pistol in the other. He did not say anything but was staring intently at her appearing to be angry. She remembers most that his eyes were black and did not move. She remembers that he had a small mustache and that his hair was dark. He had on a dark jacket and dark pants. He finally spoke telling her not to move or he would kill her. Literally jumping out of her shoes, she turned and ran from the fire to the beach house. She found her cousin and told him about the incident. They walked out on the porch, could see the fire but nothing else. They debated telling the others and calling the police but knew that it would break up the party and possibly leave some doubt as to the truth of her story. They did not tell the others and did not make a report.

Two days after Jane Hart had visited Detectives Bartey and Smith, Millie Simpson called in and stated that she wished to give information that might bear on the Borgni case. She wrote out the following report.

"I work days at the Pink Stork Club on Reynolds Street. Approximately two years ago I was working at the North Shore Lounge on Bay Street. One night a guy was in the club, and he gave me a ride home. He was about five feet, nine inches, in height with black hair and a small mustache and wore cut off pants. He was real polite and didn't drink much. When he got me home, he pushed me in the door and started choking me. He ripped my blouse off, but he did not try to rape me. He picked up a knife one time, but put it down. He jacked off on my legs and then ripped a piece off my bed sheet and started to tie my wrists, but I started laughing at him and he didn't finish tying my wrists. He didn't make me do anything to him, and he didn't feel me up any. I am almost sure that he is the same man I saw on the TV and in the paper."

Four days later a report was received from Detective Ford in Johns River, New Jersey, requesting information on Borgni. He stated that he was investigating two unsolved homicides in his area that involved two young white females. One was fourteen years old who had been raped and strangled and left half nude in a wooded area. The homicide had occurred on January 27, 1974. The second victim was an eighteen-year-old white female who had been partially disrobed and strangled with a belt but apparently had not been raped. The second victim had been killed on February 26, 1974. Detective Ford requested information on Borgni including a photograph, which was sent by the Detriville Metropolitan Police Department. No further report was ever received from Detective Ford.

Two hours later on the same day the following report was received from Jim Norton of the Federal Bureau of Investigation. "On July 26, 1973, a seven-year-old white female left her residence on her bicycle at 3:30 p.m. to retrieve a butterfly that she had previously caught and put under a stone. She resided with her parents and younger sister on Tomi Road, Sanders, Connecticut. Her mother had given the child a white envelope in which to place the butterfly.

"When the victim had not returned to her residency by 4:00 p.m. her mother and younger sister went looking for her. They located the bicycle on Salem Road some five hundred yards distance from her residence. The bicycle was in a down position.

"The Connecticut State Police instituted an immediate investigation and with the assistance of some one thousand volunteers searched the wooded area in the vicinity for a five mile radius. The victim was not located and no physical evidence recovered, including the white envelope given to the victim by her mother. New Haven followed the Connecticut State Police investigation closely for any further developments as a missing persons case. New Haven forwarded to each continental office a Connecticut State Police poster bearing the victim's photograph. A missing person notice was placed in the Identification Division. On February 8, 1974, the Department of

Justice requested the Federal Bureau of Investigation to institute an active kidnapping investigation in this matter. The White House and a number of congressmen have inquired concerning the case. Jane Kitt is described as follows:

| | |
|---|---|
| Race | White |
| Sex | Female |
| Date of Birth | 10/15/65 |
| Place of Birth | Manchester, Connecticut |
| Height | 4' |
| Weight | 65 lbs. |
| Hair | Blonde, in pigtails |
| Eyes | Blue |
| Complexion | Light |

At the time of her disappearance she was wearing a blue and white striped short sleeve pullover, navy blue shorts, with a star and flag emblem, white socks and blue sneakers. The victim's dental chart is available in New Haven."

Again, on the same day, a telephone message was received from Captain Frederick of Newton, Massachusetts, regarding two young girls who had been killed by multiple stab wounds two years previously.

On the following day Sergeant Sunny of the Key West, Florida Police Department, reported that one year previously two white female hitchhikers had been killed and dumped ninety-five miles away. Both had been shot with .22 caliber pistol bullets in the head and partially buried. One was nude except for a halter and one was fully clothed with bite marks on both breasts. His inquiry was to request information about the possibility of Borgni having been in that area at that time.

On the following day, Robert Staple of the New York State Police called requesting information on Borgni's possible presence in Westchester County in 1969. At that time a young white female had been tied, placed in a sleeping bag and thrown off a cliff. She was found eighteen months later. The one-half-inch rope and peculiar knots had been saved as evidence.

During the second week, two reports were received from the Bakersfield Police Department in Massachusetts. A routine inquiry had been made to Bakersfield to research any records on Borgni at the time that he lived in Bakersfield. The following reports were received.

At 5:15 am Officer Shaw was patrolling and received a call to go to 24 Main Street. It was stated that a woman had cut her wrists. As he approached the address, he observed a woman in her nightgown running to the telephone booth outside Homons Station. When he got to her, she was trying to get inside of the telephone booth slashing at her husband with a knife. The husband, from inside the booth, told the officer to be careful, that his wife might turn on him. As the officer was talking to the woman, he noticed that there was no flow of blood coming from either wrist and attempted to try to quiet her down. Sergeant Camp and Sergeant Westley arrived and took the woman to the hospital. Officer Shaw interviewed the husband. The husband, Mr. Borgni, explained that it was a lover's argument and that his wife would be fine. They had three children, two boys from her previous marriage and a six-month-old daughter who is their mutual child. Mrs. Borgni had previously been married to a man in the Navy and had gotten a divorce and married Mr. Borgni a year after the divorce. They had been married for one year. Mr. Borgni worked at Transeal. At 6:30 a.m. Sergeant Camp and Sergeant Westley returned and asked Mr. Borgni to go with them to the hospital to visit with his wife. They stated that she wanted to see her husband. Apparently, the wife had stated that her husband was of a strange character and background. When the officers left with Mr. Borgni, Officer Shaw stayed to oversee the care of the children. He noted in every room numerous burned out candles. He also noted a bamboo pole with an attached leather thong that apparently was a whip. There were many magazines displaying women torturing women, men torturing men, women torturing men, etc. He also came across books with titles denoting sadism and torture. There were many books of sexual esoterica. Officer Shaw formed the opinion that both parties were in a pact of strange and unusual circumstances that included self-torture. It was noted that the wife had left a written statement recently in case of an accident to her, that the police should inform her parents whose names, addresses and telephone numbers were stated. The report terminates with the fact that both Mr. and Mrs. Borgni agreed to see a physician in Stoneham, and there is a recommendation that a civic organization oversee the proper care and safety of the children.

The second report from the Bakersfield Police was written up in official form was Case # 10086. This is a complaint received by the Bakersfield Police, specifically Officer Burbage, by telephone at approximately 4:20 p.m. on April 18, 1983. The person rendering the telephone call to Officer Burbage was Clayton Sexton. Mr. Sexton was a janitor a the Vocational High School in Bakersfield. Shortly after

Mr. Sexton's call to Officer Burbage, Officer James was notified of the complaint and went to the Vocational High School. He ascertained at that place that two girls had walked out of the Bakersfield Park with their hands tied behind them. They had been picked up by an automobile on a road in the Bakersfield Park and brought to the high school. One of the girls was fully clothed. The other was clothed only in a sweater and both of them had their hands tied behind them. Shortly after Officer James arrival, Chief Winters arrived and the two of them took the girls back into the woods where they had been picked up by the automobile. By radio telephone, they learned that a third girl had wandered into a nearby campsite. She was only partially clothed and her hands were also tied. The girls gave the following account of events.

They stated that they were all in the eighth grade in a Catholic school in Ramport. They frequently had picnics together, and on this day they had left at about 12:30 p.m. on their bicycles with a picnic lunch that they intended to eat in the Bakersfield Park. As they were entering the road that leads to the beach at the Park, a small, dark car was seen behind them, and they pulled off to the side of the road to let it pass. It did not pass, so they continued with the car behind them for some distance. When they again looked for it, it apparently had turned off, and they did not see the car again. They began with their picnic lunch on a pier in the lake area. They spotted some boys across the lake and called to them to ask if they had any water to drink. The boys invited them to come around the end of the lake to their camp. At this time they noticed a man walking on the beach, and he passed the girls several times without speaking. As the girls began their trip around the end of the lake, the man stepped out of the woods and told them that the path that they were on was the wrong one and to go to the other side of the lake. He showed them a path that led deeper into the woods, which he stated was the correct path. As they proceeded down the path, Louise Charles was bringing up the rear. When they were fairly deep into the woods, Louise was suddenly grabbed from behind and a small knife was held against her neck. The three girls were told that if they made any noise the assailant would kill Louise. They were told to lie face down, and he tied their hands and feet with a white cord taken from a brown paper bag. He then gagged all three with cloth that he took from the bag. He took Rose Heath aside and untied her. He made her take all of her clothes off, and she did so. He felt her all over and then withdrew a toilet type of plunger from the paper bag. The plunger had a short handle which was green in color, and the plunger was brownish rubber in appearance. He stuck the plunger handle into her vagina. He then took Rose back to where the other two were tied and retied her and then took Louise with him. He untied her and made her strip her clothes. He gave her a small pair of underpants but found that they were too small for her and then produced another similar pair. He made her put these on. He then took the plunger and thrust the handle into her vagina. After doing so, he took her to a small pond and pushed her head under water. Thereafter, she only remembers running through the woods until she came to the camping site. While the assailant was attacking Louise, the two other girls were able to work the gags out of their mouths, and Mary Percy remembered that she had a knife in her pocket. Working together, the two girls were able to cut the cord from their legs. They began running with their hands still tied behind them. Rose was still undressed but she managed to pick up her sweater as they began running. They ran to the road where they were picked up by an automobile and taken to the school.

They described the assailant as being dressed in black dungarees, a light blue shirt and brown suede boots. They estimated his age at twenty to twenty-four years. They described his build as being medium, and that he had dark black hair that covered his ears and was curly on the ends. The hair was clean, and the assailant had a dark complexion with no observable scars or marks on his face. He was smooth shaven. They all noted that he had dark eyes. All of the material had been produced from a brown paper bag that appeared new. The pieces of cloth that he used were clean, and the knife was not seen. He mentioned stealing a car. His speech was normal, and he was not vocally abusive.

The girls were taken to be examined by a doctor where it was noted that they all had rope burns on their wrists and that the two who had been undressed had numerous scratches and welts made from running through the woods. Louise's hair was noted to be caked with leaves and wet mud and her feet were muddy. Louise said that the man had thrown her into a large puddle of water and had tried to drown her by stepping on her head. Just as she thought she was going to die, he stopped, and she rose to see him chasing the other two girls through the woods. She ran the other way and luckily into the boys' campsite. They clothed her and brought her to her house. Her parents called the police. The man was never found.

Reports continued. Each afternoon, Mrs. Barr would close the library at five, drive to the police station, and carefully sift each day's data. She and Bill Smith would then begin the tedious process of logically correlating, collating, and storing the information. When their methodologies varied or provided contest, Smith would suggest a cup of coffee. Mrs. Barr would state that she preferred tea and both would then begin the tedious process of negotiating the best method for the filing of the intelligence information.

As they worked tediously, Smith gradually learned a bit about Mrs. Barr. Good detective that he was, he knew how to start a conversation and then listen, carefully. She told him that she had fallen in love with her husband partially because of his intellect, his appreciation of the quiet life and a longtime devotion to her. She admitted, however, that her life as a librarian coupled with her habit of reading adventure and drama had left a void, a yearning for a little more excitement than she had experienced. She said that working with the police provided some of that excitement, and she felt very good at being a bit helpful in ridding society of those who hurt others.

Smith profited by learning how librarians organized and stored information. Together they produced a formidable file.

The trial came in June. The picking of the jury was tedious. It was obvious that the prosecutor was trying to seat as many women and mothers as possible and men who appeared to be willing to deal with murder. The defense seemed to be resigned to pleading a cause of mental illness. A well-known psychiatrist testified that Borgni was not insane, knew right from wrong, and was mentally capable of standing trial. The courtroom was tense. It was a large courtroom, adorned with the windows, benches, desks and tables of rich history. It was packed, but completely hushed each time Borgni was brought in and seated. The tenseness was tinged with anger and pent up hate. The crowd seemed to feel that they were viewing a monster, a monster who seldom moved during the entire process and who said nothing.

The prosecution began with the Clair/Lawton missing person reports. The anguish of not knowing where their children were, whether alive or dead, the growing apprehension of their deaths without the knowledge of where they might be was overwhelming.

The events that led to their eventually being found were carefully portrayed using the files of Smith and Mrs. Barr. Photographs of their grave sites were shown and carefully screened photographs of their bound hands and ankles were used. The hard evidence of the material used to bind and strangle them and the FBI reports that this material matched the same materials taken from Borgni's house was cement.

Finally, the psychiatric report was rendered portraying Borgni as a person who responded to unknown inner stimulations associated with the need to produce fear, terror, and death of young females was power in the hands of the prosecutors.

The door was closed on Borgni by using his own confession.

No trips were made to the Brady case or to the assaults. The prosecution stuck to a simple direct attack.

Twelve men and women returned a murder verdict within twelve hours. These were two successes on the part of the defense. One was that Borgni received a penalty of two successive life sentences instead of death and the other was that he could eventually attain the ability to plead parole.

A few days later, Borgni was transferred in chains to the State Central Prison.

# Chapter XVIII

Eight years after the trial, at the request of Dr. Andrew Stevenson, Barringer called Detective Bartey into his office and asked him to sit down.

"Bob, you remember the Borgni case?"

"Yes, sir."

"Want you to go talk to Borgni."

Absolute silence. Bartey began to slump into his chair.

Barringer hastened on. "Dr. Stevenson has an interest in him, in his violence, wants to use him as an example, maybe for some sort of program."

"On violence?" Bartey sat up.

"Yeah, maybe."

"What's he want?"

"As he expressed it," Barringer replied, "he wants to get under his skin, whatever that means. From talking to him, he believes that Borgni represents something pretty classic on the violence scene. More than that he believes that we're gonna have a lot more violence in the future. He's tinkering with the idea of trying to educate people about the forces that constitute violence and believes that Borgni is a good teaching tool."

"Dr. Stevenson's kinda weird isn't he, Captain?"

"Yes, Bob, but seldom wrong."

"I know. What do you have in mind?"

The captain and the detective talked for another hour. Barringer told Bartey most of the conversation that he had with Dr. Stevenson. He then suggested several ways to initiate the interview.

"If you can ever get Borgni to started talking, you'll have a hard time turning him off. You're gonna have to be subtle, though. He will never understand why we want to talk to him after all this time unless you're absolutely level with him."

"You mean even tell him about Dr. Stevenson?"

"No, we don't talk about Dr. Stevenson to anybody."

"What do you mean about leveling then?"

Barringer always delighted in Bartey's directness. It saved a lot of time and one seldom ever had any doubt left. "I mean be truthful with him. Tell him we're interested in his contributing to the world, maybe through a book. Tell him the subject is violence and we want to use him as an example. Be straight with him."

"I'll give it a try, kinda hard though, playing it all straight."

Both men laughed. That afternoon Barringer arranged the time and date of the first interview at the prison in the state capital.

A week later, Detective Robert Bartey, armed with legal pads, ball point pens, a tape recorder, several tapes and a small camera, left for the capital. It was the spring of 1981, the day was beautiful, and he enjoyed the two-hour drive. From the prison grounds, he entered a long, wide, underground, concrete tunnel. It let into a large reception room where he was required to produce identification and sign in. After careful scrutiny he was directed toward a set of heavy steel bar doors. Several uniformed guards sat behind a heavy bullet-proof glass window and again visually inspected him. On a signal from the first guard, electric buttons were pushed and the heavy doors opened. Bartey was asked to wait outside a small conference room. In a few minutes, Albert Borgni was brought in handcuffs chained to his waist and shuffling along in leg manacles. Bartey watched as Borgni was released. He was hardly recognizable as the man he had helped arrest eight years previously.

He was wasted, apparently by drugs. His hair was long and stringy. His face alternately twitched, grimaced, smiled in a sad way. He appeared extremely nervous. His pallor contrasted with the faded orange prison uniform he wore. He looked at Bartey in an unrecognizable fashion.

"I am Robert Bartey. I am a detective with the Detriville Metropolitan Police Department. I helped to arrest you eight years ago. I would appreciate talking to you for a little. Can we sit down in there?" Bartey motioned to the small conference room and the two went in and sat opposite each other at the small table.

"Now I remember you. I knew you were familiar, but I couldn't place you. You were with the big captain, the one with the scar on his face."

"That's right."

"What is it you want?"

The two men talked to each other for an hour. First Bartey found that Borgni was apparently a drug dealer in the prison and had become an addict. He was involved in a prison drug war and had been recently found to have a knife in his room. He was under room arrest, which explained the shackles and his dejected and despondent attitude. Bartey made the best he could of the situation and carefully explained his need of information. He stated that the information would be used to construct a real example of violence and hopefully to teach others how to avoid Borgni's present situation. With that, Borgni looked searchingly at Bartey and, finally satisfied, agreed to a series of interviews.

Bartey began slowly and unobtrusively.

"Why are you in chains?"

"Had some trouble."

"Like what?"

"They found a knife in my cell."

"Yours?"

"Yeah."

"Had some trouble?"

"Yeah. Like drugs, you know. Lots of stuff in here."

"Was it the same thing last year when they sent you back to the Institute?"

"No, that was political, had something to do with this murder thing. They sent me back over there and the people there raised hell, saying I wasn't supposed to be there, that they didn't want me so I got sent back over here."

"Why didn't they want you over there?"

"Something about this murder thing, the fact that they were little girls. That my being there would cause trouble and that they weren't as able to handle trouble as over here."

"How long you been into this drug thing?"

"Good while. You gotta do something."

"Okay, Albert, for all that. My reason for being here is to try to understand you and the reasons for all this murder thing. Maybe by understanding, we can help somebody else. Are you up to my probing around in your life a little?"

"Yeah. You know, I'm really sorry about all that happened. I wish it hadn't."

"Have you been seen by a shrink since you've been in?"

"No, and I've wondered about that. Nobody in this hole needed a shrink more than I did when I came in, but, no, no shrink."

"Did you ask for one?"

"No."

"Has there been anybody you could talk to?"

"No, except my cell mate, we talk a lot."

"What's his name?"

"Jim."

"What's he in for?"

"Manslaughter."

"Have you told him about this murder thing?"

"No, not really, he wouldn't understand, he's kinda dumb, big macho complex, that why he killed the guy he's in for."

"Can you talk to me?"

"Yeah, maybe. Nobody can do any more to me that has already been done and they can't convert my sentence. My only hope is parole."

"You know I can't make a deal?"

"Yeah, but maybe, shoot."

"Do you really regret what you've done?"

"Yeah. Having time to mull the whole thing over, without any type of counseling or real interest being shown by anyone, yeah. Not regrets that I got caught, but regrets for things that occurred. If there was a way to undo it, I wish it could have been undone."

"Why do you think you did what you did?"

"I don't know. A spell would come over me, and I couldn't resist it. I had visions of how young girls would look, how scared they could get and how being bound up and helpless would make them look."

"Why young girls?"

"They are easy, young, vulnerable, scared. I needed to humiliate, degrade the people involved."

"Why?"

"I don't know."

"Was it sexual?"

"No, not really. It was more of an emotional thing. Something that lay dormant for a while and then would rise up inside of me, like kind of a need. I didn't know what it was, what caused it or when it was coming. All I do know is that it has been there all of my life, even before I knew what sex was."

"Did you eventually get sexual satisfaction from it?"

"No. Sometimes sex got mixed up in it but when it was all over I was drained of everything, afraid, apprehensive, nervous. I couldn't do anything."

"What was it then, if sex wasn't behind it, what did you get out of it?"

"I don't know. What I do know is that once the fire in me started, it wouldn't go out until it went away by itself. I had no control over myself. I had no choice."

"Well, why did you spare some of them?"

"Either they didn't fit or the circumstances didn't fit."

"What do you mean by that?"

"Well, in the case of the girl who fingered me, she wouldn't get scared, she even offered herself to me, it took away the feeling."

"You mean she didn't fit the picture of fear and humiliation?"

"Yeah."

"And you are telling me that you had this need even when you were young, before puberty?"

"No. When I was young I didn't have the feelings, only the pictures. I had pictures in my head. Later when I discovered them in magazines, I collected them and would actually study them. I became a student of bondage even at a young age."

"But you didn't feel anything then?"

"No. It's like looking at something is all you need. Your mind goes blank. You can look at it for hours. It's why children hurt animals. They just want to see. They don't feel the pain, they just want to see. There are plenty of people here in the can who never think. They just like to see. To watch. No matter what."

Bartey knew that Borgni had relaxed and appeared to be enjoying talking with someone other than his cell mate. He steered the conversation to Borgni's youth. Borgni told him that he had been severely constrained by his mother. His mother had objected to most of his friends, had kept him home most of his early years. She had objected to all girlfriends, stating that they were dirty and only wanted to have sex with him. Borgni stated that he felt he had been emotionally abused.

Bartey asked, "Did she ever sexually abuse you?"

Borgni replied, "Not in a sexual sense. There were times when she would—I'd be taking a bath or something like that, and she'd come walking into the bathroom and remark how manly I was looking. Or there would be times when I'd just be standing around the house and she'd come out of the clear blue sky, come up and pinch you on the rear end or grab you by the nuts and say, 'Oh wow, you are really growing up.'"

"So you think you hated her at that time?"

"I think, yes."

"Al, did you ever have trouble with the cops when you were young?"

"Well, here's where we run into a problem. It was strictly on an impulse, on a lark. Let's see. I was about fourteen, and I was down by what we called the Green, which was the little shopping center in the area, and there was this girl, and it was just on an impulse and I said well I'm just going to scare the hell out of her and just take her bike and leave it two blocks down. And I had a little pocket knife. So I took the pocket knife out and said, 'I'm going to take your bike away.' And just as I was doing that her mother came out of the house. They happened to be living just across the street. Then her dad came out of the house, got hold of me, and called the police. So the police came down, and I was arrested and taken to headquarters and charged with being a juvenile delinquent and put on probation. I think it was six months. And that's the only run-in with the law."

"That's the first time?"

"The first time."

"Do you think there was any significance to the knife and the fact that she was a girl?"

"Perhaps."

"Do you think that set a pattern?"

"It may have. It may have been a sign of things to come."

"Did you think of that before you did it?"

"No. It was strictly an impulse at that time."

"You didn't have the knife with you for that purpose."

"No. All the guys had a pocket knife. Kind of like a status symbol."

"Was the girl somebody you knew?"

"No. She was a complete stranger."

"You were fourteen then. You were sexually capable. Did you think you were going to screw her or something?"

"No. There was no intent on that. The thought hadn't even crossed my mind."

"Why did they make such a big deal out of it?"

"Well, as I recall, the first thing that they had on their mind, you know, was that there was some sort of sexual overtone. Her parents were worried about that. There was a brief session with a psychiatrist. He asked some questions about sex but I told him that I was just playing and had no sexual intentions. They put me on probation because no one was hurt so it was just a matter of a short time on probation."

"Al, let me ask you something. When that happened, do you think there was any rebellion towards your mother?"

"Yeah. I think so. I was going through a rather rebellious kind of period. And I think, perhaps I was trying, if I had to put my finger on a motivation, that I was perhaps trying to get back subconsciously."

"Do you really believe that?"

"It kind of made me hurt her, not the girl but my mother."

"Is that stretching all you've learned about psychology too much or do you really believe that?"

"No, I don't think it stretches. I don't think so. I think subconsciously, you know what I mean? I can't say, well, I'm going to get at my mother by scaring the hell out of this girl. That's not the way the thought runs. It may have been a subconscious thought. I was just going through a rebellious period. The day I went down to the Green to hang out, and my parents said, 'The first thing you did, you went down there and you got in trouble.'"

"How about sex early on?"

"Let's see, I guess I was about sixteen when I had my first sexual experience. The girl was a year younger and when it was done, you wonder, gee, is that all there is to it? I tried to decide whether it was an emotional experience or purely a physical thing. I think, looking back, I never had any strong emotions, except during my spells. When I was a teenager, we had a little band and made some decent money. The band was the best thing of my younger life. When you are in a band, the girls are easy and I had my share. The truth is,

I didn't love any of them and the few times I brought one home, my mother made things so unpleasant, that I quit bringing them. The band was a good thing and I liked the other members but only because they were necessary to make up a band. They were so-called friends, but the truth is I didn't have any real, you know, close friends. So sex came pretty easy, and I liked it but it was a physical thing not an emotional experience. Sometimes I think I don't have any emotions at all, except during my spells. I have sometimes thought that my spells are a substitute for not having any emotions. The only emotion I can identify was my interest in bondage, and I think that is what eventually brought on my spells. In view of what has happened, I sure as hell would have liked to have had some help with that."

"When did your interest in bondage begin?"

"I guess I was probably about ten. It was in the comic books where the heroine would be tied up. For some reason I found that sort of attractive or fascinating. Never to the standpoint where I wanted to participate or do it. It was just the pictures."

"But Al, you really believe that you became attracted or focused upon bondage before puberty?"

"I think so."

"Clearly before twelve or thirteen years of age you were looking at it. What did you think about it at that time? What were the thoughts—why was this heroine, bound up, attractive to you? Why did you focus on it?"

"It was the idea of being in charge, the idea of being in total control. I've always enjoyed sex, but I'm not looking at bondage from a sexual point of view. I've always prided myself as being a person in control of himself in given situations. I was able to do the job that I had in the military, which was frequently a pressure job, and I work good under pressure. I can work good in situations of pressure where other people are kind of losing their wits, and maintain a cool disposition about it. Almost icy sort of calm, but you know sometimes very necessary."

"It is almost as if something was left out of me when I was born, you know, like what I said about emotions. For some strange reason, even before puberty, when I saw a female bound so that she had no ability to do anything, I became intensely focused. When the spell broke, I felt satisfied, satiated, and later when the spells became associated with violence and were over, I would be very weak physically, very nervous and anxious. It was like I had been through a storm quietly and in absolute control, but when it was over, I hardly had control of myself."

"What did you see when you looked at pictures of bound women?"

"At first, when I was young, I don't think I saw anything other than the picture itself. Later, I saw the obvious pain, the discomfort, the abnormal positions. Much later, I saw the terror, the dejection, the desperation, and the utter helplessness. I saw myself in complete control, and I enjoyed their terror."

"Did you ever imagine that the bound female could represent your mother?"

"I've thought about that and the answer is yes and no. It seems to me that early on, when I was a kid that the whole fascination with bondage could have started with a subconscious thought that the bound female was my mother, bound so that she couldn't tell me what to do or embarrass me, or make me feel inferior on anything. If that were the start of it, the whole thing eventually changed. When I became an adult my fascination with bondage gradually became associated with inflicting pain and pain only because it involved more terror. I gradually became focused only on very young girls because it was so easily possible to cause them to be hopelessly terrified."

"Why did you kill some of your victims when you really didn't have to?"

"I really didn't mean to, I simply went too far."

"Were your spells getting more frequent and more intense?"

"Yes."

"Have you had spells in prison?"

"No, there is nothing here to stimulate anything. Maybe that is why it was so easy for me to use drugs."

"Al, if by chance, you were to get out of prison by parole, would your spells come back and maybe cause you to hurt someone again?"

"No, because I've found God. I could never hurt anyone again."

With that Bartey reviewed the whole process of the interview. He went over every detail of Borgni's life, over his youth again in detail, of where he had lived during various stages of his life, of police reports in those other places, once all the details of Borgni's marriage, his relationship with his children, reasons for lack of close friends and specifically, the details of the death of the children at Pirates Beach.

It took three separate trips to complete the interviews.

When the last interview was over, Bartey stood up in the small room and packed his briefcase.

"So, Al, you've found God?"

"Yeah, I have."

"Well, Al, it's gonna take God to get you out of here."

Borgni managed a slight shrug, barely smiled, and offered his wrists to the security guard to be re-handcuffed.

Bartey turned and was led through the massive iron doors to the reception room, and then to the concrete tunnel and finally to fresh air.

He took a deep breath and walked to his car. As he was driving away he thought, "We should have killed the son-of-a-birth when we arrested him. He'll never get out, but if it did happen, we'll have to kill him eventually."

He stopped, got some coffee and began to plan how to organize all of his material for the captain and Dr. Stevenson.

# Epilogue

In the fall of 1983, Dr. Andrew Stevenson spun the wheel of his automobile. The car veered sharply into a right turn lane of traffic, braked quickly, and he watched several cars pass. When traffic had subsided he crossed the lanes, turned left and then into the parking lot of a restaurant, which was closed. Following a familiar but cautious routine he found Captain Barringer inside the restaurant nurturing a cup of coffee. Stevenson placed a thick manuscript on the counter.

"Andrew, you got more curiosity than is healthy."

"That a threat?"

"Only if you get too curious about me."

Both men laughed. Barringer knew that Stevenson wanted follow-up on the people involved and that he wanted to know the conclusions that Stevenson had made on the nature of violence.

"What more do you want to know, Andrew?"

"Just some follow-up. What has happened to the original team?"

"Well, Pierce is now chief over in Haynesworth and doing a good job. Calls me every once in a while when he's got a sensitive case. I'm very proud of him, and I think he's proud of himself. Fielding is still with me. He is mother hen to Canthus and Bartey, and they need it. Canthus is still dancing on his tight rope, but if he looks like he might slip you'll find Bartey and Fielding somewhere in the crowd. Woe is he who monkeys with one of the three of them. Bartey still plays with the night squirrels. He seems to understand their needs and only enforces the letter of the law. They flip to him pretty often, and it gives us a lot of info. He is married, you know. He is very quiet and soft around her, but is still a tense cat in the violent world. Ivers and Smith still maintain the intelligence file. They try to organize it well, but Mrs. Barr comes in occasionally to help them."

"What has happened to Dr. Davis?"

"He's still at the museum, 'sposed to retire each year but they say that his bones will probably go next to the dinosaurs. McCarthy is still teaching pathology at the University. He's always late to everything but is the most thorough man I know. Dr. Rider is still trying to develop psychiatric criminal profiles."

"What has he accomplished?"

"He has established a set of predictors of violence."

"Yeah, I've read his paper, let me see if I can remember. Being male, having a high testosterone level, a low serotonin level, and indulgent in alcohol and drugs. Having one parent, childhood behavior problems, childhood abuse, low verbal IQ and poverty. If the kid does poorly in school, has deviant friends, has witnessed violent acts, and has been arrested by age fourteen, all of these are predictors of becoming violent."

"Damn, Andrew, do you memorize everything you read?"

"No, they fit my need to describe different causes of violence. Oh, by the way whatever happened to the guy who found the first body?"

"Eugene Wilson. He's married now, and he and his wife raise Labrador retrievers. Best dogs you ever saw, gain strength from swimming in the surf. If you're ever out at Pirates Beach and see kids chasing black puppies, they're both probably some of the Wilson's."

"How about the girls who survived?"

"The young ones adapted well. They are lucky to be alive, and they know it. They carry scars but know that they have to live without fear so have tried to forget it all. We will always be grateful to Dori. She married the Navy guy. She had a lot of strength, and I hope life will treat her well."

"I hear Borgni is up for parole."

"Yeah, but he won't make it. Too much trouble in the can. Right or wrong, he has had no access to good psychiatric treatment. He is a lost soul."

"Guess that's what they mean by hell, huh."

"Yeah, I guess. The way I hear it, he lives just this side of hell all the time. Prison is a tough place. Some don't come out."

"Well, it's been an interesting trip."

"What did you learn?"

"Oh, I don't know. First, it seems that there are a lot of forms of violence, some of which I've never seen categorized. There are occasions where violence leads to violence, the old 'eye for an eye' routine. This is the violence of vindication, of retribution, the essence of the vendetta. Then there is the case where violence breeds violence. Most child abusers were abused as children, and Albert Borgni certainly considered himself emotionally abused. There is the case of violence being the necessary solution to violence, as in the case of police force when needed. And, finally, there seems to be an inherent uncontrolled emotional urge for violence. Boxing, football, street fights, and war seem to reflect man's inherent need for violence. They were all present in the Borgni case. His case seems to have been born in anger and developed into hate. Whether such feelings are genetically transmitted or learned is open to question. It seems that a lot of violence is born out of frustration, in people who simply don't understand situations, who have never been taught how to cope with real life. The way I see it is that our educational system teaches a lot about everything but living. We teach the anatomy of sex but not the emotion of sex. We teach social studies but not how to get along in marriage. We teach psychology out of a book but not how to deal with real people in real living situations."

"You're hung up on the educational bit again, huh?"

"Yeah I guess so. I genuinely believe that the future only belongs to those who live in it. The authors of our Constitution did a pretty good job for that era but it really doesn't suffice for us now. I am going to predict that ten years from now violence will be so prevalent that some bright people will begin to recognize that they have to face it as an issue, understand it, and teach others to understand. If I am living then, I would advocate teaching kids how to live without violence, how to truly be civilized, to have good relationships with each other. Only the kids bring hope."

"Drew, I respect your opinions, but to me violence is a part of human nature, and I doubt if you are going to change that."

Stevenson picked up the file, stood up and stretched. "Randy, I am not going to change you and don't want to." He shook the file. "But in this case violence was born, nurtured, and developed within one violent man."

"Bartey did a good job with Borgni but Borgni just doesn't fit in, anywhere. He was not nearly as abused by his mother as he implies. His early fascination with bondage is not explainable. The undeniable increase in frequency and intensity of his abnormal episodes and his increasing associated of his spells with violence and death are documented. He would have hurt and killed again and again. As to his stating that he has become religious, that is nothing more than an attempt to eventually gain a parole. Borgni is unique. There is simply something wrong with his brain, and nobody can fix it. You know how I am about trying to educate against violence, but this is one monster that courts should have sent to the electric chair. You know, occasionally, there is reason for revenge."

Barringer looked at his coffee, absent mindedly stroked the large scar on his face and nodded.